A GIRL CALLED CHANCE

Following a broken romance and a bout of pneumonia, Miss Chance Lester arrives in Yorkshire to recuperate at the home of her uncle, Dr Tobias Lester. Betsy, the cook, and Thomas, the coachman, welcome Chance, but she is received with hostility by her uncle's housekeeper, Miss Bostide and the hunchbacked little maid Eva. During her stay, Chance meets and falls in love with Dr Edward Bradle, but their relationship provokes a number of attempts on Chance's life. Many secrets must be uncovered before Chance and Edward can begin a life together.

A GIRL CALLED CHANCE

A Girl Called Chance

by

Lloyd Peters

Dales Large Print Books
Long Preston, North Yorkshire,
BD23 4ND, England.

British Library Cataloguing in Publication Data.

Peters, Lloyd
    A girl called Chance.

    A catalogue record of this book is
    available from the British Library

    ISBN   1-84262-380-X pbk

First published in Great Britain in 1978 by IPC Magazines Ltd.

Published in Large Print 2005 by arrangement with
Lloyd Peters

Dales Large Print is an imprint of Library Magna Books Ltd.

Printed and bound in Great Britain by
T.J. (International) Ltd., Cornwall, PL28 8RW

CHAPTER ONE

Miss Chance Lester stepped down from the coach that had brought her on the last stage of her journey from London to the house called Edgestones in Yorkshire. The dusk was deepening and the air felt cold.

As she paused and waited a moment, she looked about her. At the doorway, the downstairs windows with lights beginning to throw their shadows on the curtains, and at the massive stonework. She glanced upwards and found herself staring at a face framed in a corner of an upstairs window. The gaze fixed penetratingly on her was cold and hostile. In an instant the face was gone as if it had never been, and the curtain corner fluttered and fell back into place.

Chance felt a slight shock, but then she heard the coachman's deferent request for her to follow him.

A woman of about thirty-five, dressed in a black skirt and white high-necked blouse, stood in the doorway. She inclined her head and a serious smile widened her full lips.

'I am Miss Bostide, housekeeper to Dr Lester. Welcome to Edgestones, Miss Lester.'

Chance smiled in tired fashion. 'Thank you. I am pleased to be here, Miss Bostide. It has been a long journey.'

'Your room is ready. Eva will bring you water and then you can have tea.' She paused, then continued: 'Dr Lester had to go out on a call.'

For a few moments they regarded each other. There was a watchful curiosity in Miss Bostide's eyes. Her voice was of the North and not unpleasant, but Chance had discerned a certain lack of warmth in her tone.

The housekeeper was of medium height, full-figured, and her hair was dark, wiry and shortish. Her skin had a tawny sheen to it.

Her mouth was large, and her eyes appeared to be almost black. A vital life force seemed to pulsate from the older woman, before which Chance, travel weary as she was, felt drained and insipid.

Behind her the coachman shifted his feet and the housekeeper glanced at him.

'Thomas, take Miss Lester's luggage upstairs.'

They followed him along the hall which ran from the front to the back of the house with a staircase beginning half-way along it.

Ascending the stairs brought them to a large square landing with several doors opening off it.

Thomas appeared from a room on the left, and Chance could not help smiling when she looked at him. If a person could be known by a colour, he would be a brown man. From the tip of his battered high-crowned hat to the equally well-creased boots, this impression persisted.

The eyes were brown and warm and the face, of a slightly lighter hue, narrowed towards the forehead then broadened towards the cheeks to prominent stubbly jowls. His nose was short and round with a bulbous end and the overall appearance of his face suggested a jacketed potato.

He addressed Miss Bostide in a gruff broad speech. 'I'll go and put Blossom away. Good night, ma'am.' His eyes switched to Chance. 'Good night, miss.'

'Good night to you, Thomas,' replied Chance, 'and thank you for bringing me here today.'

'Oh, it were nothing.' Thomas hid his pleasure behind a cough and made his way down the stairs. He was followed by the housekeeper after she had shown Chance to her bedroom.

Chance threw open her cases but then decided to unpack later. She drew the heavy curtains apart and stood looking out into the darkness. All was quiet except for the fluttering and popping of the gas mantles, which bathed the room in a dim yellow light. How peaceful it was after the hustle and bustle of London.

She turned away from the window and was startled to find the housekeeper standing in the shadow of the doorway watching her.

'I've brought your water myself, Miss Lester. Eva is busy elsewhere,' the housekeeper explained, crossing the room and placing the jug on the washstand. On the way out again, she glanced at Chance. 'I did not mean to startle you.'

Chance gave a quick smile. 'I was busy with my thoughts.'

Miss Bostide closed the door behind her, leaving Chance with the feeling that the housekeeper had been observing her with hostility.

But, by the time she had washed, changed and made her way downstairs, the incident had gone from her mind.

In the sitting-room which was to be hers during her stay at the house, Chance sat down to a special meal with all that was the best in Yorkshire cooking.

The meal had been brought in and served by Betsy, the cook, herself. Chance liked Betsy on sight. A stout person with an enormous bosom, she was neatly dressed in a blue gown with a long apron of white. She wore a crinkled cap over her grey hair, and her blue eyes had twinkled kindly out of a warm, pink, fresh face. She was Thomas's wife.

Chance leaned back and relaxed. How cosy it was! The fire glowed and the room was comfortably furnished. She thought of the disaster that had brought her to Edge-stones … a childhood-sweetheart affair which had lasted into adulthood … her trusting and unquestioning step towards the marriage. But love, if ever it had been that, had left her sweetheart by then and the dream romance was shattered. Chance remembered the pain.

Her whole being at a low ebb, she had caught cold. Pneumonia had set in and she had hovered between life and death for days. Recovery had been slow and convalescence away from the place of unhappy memories had been suggested. Her uncle, Dr Lester, had been contacted and he had agreed to her staying with him for a month or so. What better hands could she be in?

And here she was.

There was a knock on her door and it opened. She turned in her chair to find the very person she had been thinking about standing there – her uncle, Dr Tobias Lester.

'Uncle Toby,' she exclaimed gladly, getting up and going towards him with hands outstretched in greeting.

'Chance, my dear girl, it is so good to see you.'

She kissed him on both cheeks, smelling the tobacco on his clothes from the pipe which he habitually smoked. Tall, spare, long nosed, with bushy side-whiskers, his head was bald except for a few strands of hair criss-crossing the top of it.

He stepped back and surveyed her face with searching kindliness from under straggling eyebrows. 'And how are you truly, Chance?'

'Feeling better already.' She smiled then added: 'If I continue to have meals the size of the one I've just eaten, I shall return to London looking somewhat like your cook.'

Her uncle nodded. 'She's a treasure. I gave her orders that she was to feed you well. Weakness breeds despondency.'

'Have you eaten yet, Uncle?' she asked.

'No, I came straight in to see you, but I'm used to odd meal times.'

Chance glanced at the table. 'There is tea left in the pot and it is still warm. Have a cup with me now.'

'Very well, I will.' He accepted her offer in pleased fashion. 'There is no need for me to hurry now.'

Chance poured a cup of tea for him and he drank it with an appreciative smack of the lips. Then he looked directly across at her.

'What manner of man was he – the rogue who let you down so badly?' He checked himself, then went on: 'Sorry, Chance. It was thoughtless of me, bringing the matter up, but really...' He shrugged as if mystified.

She smiled, shaking her head. 'I'm all right now, I'm over it. I can look at the matter and realise how foolish I was.'

Dr Lester toyed with his cup as he observed his niece discreetly. It was five years since he'd seen her. Fair-haired, open-faced, pale of skin – more so now, he guessed, because of her recent illness. Twenty-three she would be soon. Her blue eyes gave her nature away. They were sensitive, loyal.

His mind went back to his London practice, before he had come to Yorkshire. He remembered the despair in his brother and sister-in-law at their childless condition, and how he had brought them a baby girl to adopt. He had been told of the unwanted child while on his rounds one day.

He heard again the words of the intermediary between himself and the unknown parent:

'It's what I call a chance child, Dr Lester. Came too late in life, and isn't wanted. Came just by chance.'

And that tiny bundle had grown into the woman seated before him…

For a while Chance and her uncle talked. She found out that the housekeeper, Miss Bostide, had worked at Edgestones for about fifteen years, and had lived here for three of them. She was separated from her husband, who owned the White Eagle Inn on the edge of the moors. Eva, the maid Chance had not yet met, had been at the house for twelve years.

During the course of the conversation, Chance was a little surprised to find that her uncle seemed reluctant to discuss Miss Bostide. She wondered why.

Dr Lester finally pushed himself to his feet. 'I'd best be going, my dear Chance, otherwise the worthy Betsy will leave my service. She takes it to heart if I do not do justice to her splendid cooking.'

He looked down at his niece and went on:

'Truth to tell, at the end of the day when I sit down, I don't want to get up again. One of these days I shall hand over the reins to Dr Bradle, and take a back seat.'

'Dr Bradle?' questioned Chance in surprise.

'My partner. I took him into the practice some six months ago. A nice young man, and he will make a good doctor when I've finished with him.' He paused and stared at her. 'You haven't met yet?'

She shook her head. 'No, the only other man I've met is Thomas.'

'Ah, Thomas. A rare old character.' He moved towards the door then turned back again. 'As your physician, my dear, a prescription of a week of early nights will be the correct medicine.'

She laughed lightly. 'I shall try to be a most obedient patient, Uncle Toby.'

'When there is understanding between patient and doctor all will be well.' He opened the door and went on: 'Thank you for the tea, Chance. It has pleased me greatly to see you again. I'm not far away. My room is at the front on this side.'

The door closed and she heard his footsteps go down the hall. She sat down again, thinking what a pleasant man her uncle was. Not a cuddly sort of uncle, but she'd always been fond of him.

She decided to read for a while. She had brought a few books with her, but they were still packed in the cases in her bedroom.

The hall was empty and the house was quiet as she went upstairs. She collected her books and, while doing so, gave a backward glance at the door, remembering how earlier the figure of the housekeeper standing there had startled her.

Holding her books, she began to descend the stairs. Half-way down, one of them escaped her grasp and landed with a flat cracking sound a few steps below. Chance bent down and retrieved the book. On straightening, instinct made her glance up the stairs and she jumped. She was being silently watched again, but by someone else.

She found herself looking into the face she had seen at the window on arriving at the house. The pale eyes staring into hers were no friendlier than before. Underneath them, the nose and mouth were small, and a framework of golden hair fell around the pale skin.

She moved and Chance saw that she was not only tiny but deformed, having a hunched back. Chance guessed she was about twenty-five.

Deciding to be as pleasant as possible despite the other's unwelcoming stare, Chance smiled and asked: 'Is your name Eva?'

'Yes.' The voice was high pitched and shrill, and she did not look at Chance.

'I am Miss Lester.'

'I know.' For a moment the eyes glanced up, then away again.

Abruptly she brushed past Chance and went down the stairs, the distorted body carried on legs which took little impatient steps along the hall to disappear into the farthest room on the right. This room, Chance was to learn later, was the house-keeper's.

Back in her sitting-room, Chance placed her books on the table thoughtfully, puzzling over her brief meeting with Eva. What was the reason for the maid's resentful and impolite manner?

For about an hour she read but then her drooping eyelids told her it was time for bed.

After going along to her uncle's room and wishing him good night, she walked towards the stairs. She heard the front door open behind her and glanced back as a man entered the house.

Putting down a small dark case, he flung his hat and coat on the hallstand impatiently. It was then that he noticed Chance standing there. She saw him start slightly, then frown as he stared at her.

'You will be Miss Lester?'

Chance took a step towards him. 'Yes, I'm Dr Lester's niece.'

She smiled and offered her hand, which he took, saying: 'Dr Bradle. You will forgive the coldness of my hand but travelling in a trap on a chilly night is no way to keep warm.'

'It is I who must apologise. I think I startled you.'

'Coming home in the dark, Miss Lester, after a long day, causes a man to see all sorts of things which are not there.' Dr Bradle's eyes smiled into her. 'For a moment I thought you were one of those flights of fancy, but pleasanter than most.'

Chance took her gaze away form her companion. She felt in some extraordinary way that although they had only just met, she and this man had conversed many times together.

He passed a hand in tired fashion over his eyes.

Chance said apologetically: 'You must be weary. I had no right to engage you in conversation so late.'

'It is the shortening days and lengthening nights that tire me, not our conversation,

21

Miss Lester.' He smiled regretfully and continued: 'Winter starts early up here and seems to go on a long time.'

The lemon-coloured gaslight revealed Dr Bradle as a man of about twenty-six, tall and wiry rather than thin. He had dark straight hair, grey eyes, and eyebrows with a slight upwards slant. His nose was broad with a slight hook to it.

'Have you eaten yet, Dr Bradle?' she asked.

'No, but Betsy will have left something in the oven for me. A good woman, but I cannot expect her to wait all night for me. She likes to go home sometimes.'

'Then I will get it for you,' said Chance.

'No.' He put out a hand. 'I do thank you for your consideration, but you are here to convalesce not to act as a skivvy.'

She laughed. 'Hardly a skivvy, Dr Bradle, setting out one meal.'

'Nevertheless, I cannot allow it. Hannah – Miss Bostide – or Eva will see to it for me.' He took a step towards his room then looked back at her. 'How long will you be staying in Edgestones, Miss Lester?'

'I don't know, but about a month.'

'Then we shall have the opportunity to talk again.'

'I hope so, Dr Bradle. Good night.'

'Good night, Miss Lester.'

She turned to make her way along the hall, noticing that the housekeeper's door was open slightly. As she mounted the stairs slowly, feeling weary now, she heard it close.

She went to bed recalling the kindly welcome of four of the household and the strange behaviour of the other two – Miss Bostide, and Eva of the mask-like face and tortured body.

She fell into a fitful sleep and dreamed that she was being chased by Eva urged on by the housekeeper. A man appeared in front of her. She was swept into his arms … out of danger. She held him tightly and looked up at him.

It was Dr Bradle. Then the face faded and

Chance awoke to find herself clutching a pillow.

After a breakfast which left no doubt in Chance's mind that her stomach would be well looked after during her stay, she explored the outside of the house. The day was cold but a bright sun took some of the sorrow of autumn away.

She saw Thomas, his shirtsleeves rolled to the elbow, making a pile of leaves ready for burning. He touched his forelock and called a greeting on seeing her. Chance had liked Thomas at their first meeting.

At the end of the drive, Winter Hill – a steep lane up which she had come from Allcaster – continued past the gates towards the moors near by. Dark outcrops of rock jutted against the skyline, brooding, over-looking. She wondered if the name of the house was derived from these.

She strolled round to the rear of the house, noticing a path which led at a less steep angle to the moors. Across the large cobbled courtyard were the stables. Betsy had told her that two horses were kept. Blossom, who had brought her in the coach yesterday, and Apple, a black mare.

Chance retraced her steps to the front, where Thomas pushed a bunch of roses into her hands.

In his broad dialect, punctuated as usual by his chuckle-cum-cough, he told her they would brighten up her room. The roses would, he thought, be the last good ones of the summer.

He appeared embarrassed at her appreciative thanks, shrugged them away and bent again to his work.

Chance entered the house. She saw that the housekeeper's door was open. Perhaps Miss Bostide would have a vase, and possibly she would like to have some of the flowers. Chance knocked and waited. There was no answer. She pushed the door open gently and looked in, but the room was unoccupied.

Not wanting anyone to think she was prying, she re-entered the hall and closed the door behind her, pausing to smell the roses.

'Miss Bostide's gone out.'

Chance looked up sharply. Eva stood near the kitchen, her eyes cold and suspicious.

'I – I wondered if Miss Bostide had a vase for the flowers,' Chance said hesitantly, feeling rather guilty.

She smiled at the small figure. The maid's expression did not alter. She nodded towards the kitchen.

'Ask her, she might have one.'

With that she disappeared into Dr Lester's room and Chance, entering the kitchen, heard his door being closed with more force than was necessary. She felt irritated at Eva's incivility, but Betsy's invitation to have a mid-morning cup of tea and a slice of freshly-baked fatty cake soon restored her equanimity.

Later, as she sat before the fire, the thought came that although she had not yet been at Edgestones twenty-four hours, it had already supplied her with a few surprises.

But the days passed by pleasantly. Sometimes Chance would take the path from the side of the house to the edge of the moors, gain her breath and look across the valley with its fields and black stone walls. At other times she would go down into the village to shop.

Occasionally she would accompany her uncle on his rounds, and once Thomas took her with him into Allcaster.

And Chance began to feel much better. The pink was returning to her cheeks and her clothes were fitting better. Now and then Betsy could be seen discreetly observing the satisfactory results of her cooking.

The attitudes of the other two women in the house towards Chance altered very little during this time. Eva maintained her offhanded cold manner and Miss Bostide remained formal and polite.

Of Dr Bradle Chance saw little in that first week. He would be gone by the time she breakfasted. Sometimes she saw him from her bedroom window as he set out, often accompanied by Thomas.

When Chance did meet Dr Bradle around the house, he would pass the time of day and enquire after the progress of her health. And always his eyes seemed to look into her very mind. Perhaps, she thought, it was a habit he'd got into through studying his patients to see what lay behind their faces.

On his return from his morning round one day, she chanced to meet him in the hallway outside Miss Bostide's door. After a few moments of conversation between them, the door opened and she saw the flash of annoyance in the housekeeper's face at seeing them together...

As Chance went up to bed that night, she saw Dr Bradle enter Miss Bostide's room without knocking. He did not see Chance in the gloom of the stairs, but to her he had the air of a man who had done that very thing many times.

The next morning Chance was awakened by the sound of the church bells ringing to summon people to early Communion.

Later, Chance went to morning service. She walked down Winter Hill and saw the tumbling water of the stream splashing down the small ravine to one side of it.

She sat at the back of the church, but many were the curious glances cast at the fair-haired young woman. The church was cold and she shivered a little as she prayed and gave thanks that her health was returning.

And, although Chance would not have admitted to doing so, a small separate voice sent up a request for Dr Bradle to notice her a little more.

After the service she made her way outside quickly, thinking that the walk up Winter Hill would soon make her warm again. Nearing the church gates she was pleasantly surprised to see Dr Bradle and Thomas approaching in the trap. They stopped and waited.

'Good morning, Miss Lester,' Dr Bradle called to her, taking off his hat. 'Are you going back to the house?'

'Good morning to you, Dr Bradle. Yes, I

am.' She added, looking up at him. 'But I can walk.'

'It's a long and tiring climb.'

With that he stepped down and offered his hand to help Chance into the trap.

At that moment, the vicar detached himself from the centre of a group of women parishioners, and bounced rather than walked up to them.

Thomas gave one of his coughs, and Chance saw him shoot a wearied glance of resignation at Dr Bradle.

The vicar exchanged a few pleasantries with Dr Bradle, who then introduced Chance to him. The Reverend Percy Trupple was a short round man who exuded an energy which could almost be felt, and his habit of swaying backwards and forwards made Chance think that he was likely to leap somewhere at any moment. His handshake was firm and warm.

'You must have great faith in our good doctors to come so far,' he said, smiling kindly. 'Your uncle is a very worthy man.

My best wishes for regaining your full health, and perhaps you will also join our congregation again?'

'Thank you, Vicar. No doubt you will see me a few times before I return to London.'

'That is good to hear, Miss Lester,' he said, turning to regard Thomas.

The coachman was perched up on his seat, elbows on knees, staring straight ahead and obviously hoping that the vicar's keen eyes would by some miracle fail to see him.

The vicar continued thoughtfully: 'After all these years in this parish I'm still trying to bring the word of God to some of the heathen. We do need the older members of the community to be present in order to steady the faith of the young and show the way to the ungodly.'

Thomas coughed and looked very uncomfortable.

'Well, Vicar, what with one thing and t'other…'

Chance saw that he was in difficulties, but Dr Bradle came to his aid swiftly.

'I think what Thomas means, Vicar, is that Dr Lester and myself have left him very little free time recently.'

The vicar nodded, but fixed his gaze on Thomas again.

'Your service, Thomas, to the doctors is very praiseworthy, but we must not forget to serve also our Master above, who expects a little of our time.'

His eyes, to Thomas's relief, looked away as he said: 'Even the most saintly of us can fall. My predecessor was a fine man but he was tempted with the bottle.' He pointed to a corner of the cemetery. 'He's resting over there now, and not likely to get anything stronger than water.'

His eyes fairly danced in his round face, and Chance was amused and surprised at this display of macabre humour from a man of the Church.

Dr Bradle said, to Chance's relief, for she was now feeling colder: 'I think, Vicar, that we're both nearing the end of our morning's work. I have another call to make, if you will excuse me.'

'Of course, Doctor,' beamed the Reverend Percy Trupple. With that, he made his way back to the circle of women waiting to enclose him.

Dr Bradle helped Chance up into the trap and insisted that she tuck a rug around herself.

With Chance on one side and Dr Bradle on the other, Thomas flipped the reins. It was some quarter of an hour later when Chance was set down at the gates of the house, and the trap continued upwards towards the moors.

She walked along the drive to the front door. As she did so, Miss Bostide watched from her room, and Chance would have been surprised at the look of displeasure on her face.

During the third week of her stay at Edgestones, Chance was told by Thomas that there was to be a bonfire to celebrate November the Fifth in the yard at the rear of the house, and the local people would be invited.

By Friday evening, a mountainous cone of wood had arisen in the yard. When Chance went out to join those already present, the air was heavy with smoke from a dozen or more fires blazing and there were excited murmurings as the first flames spread.

There were lots of children and adults around the fire. Chance noticed some onlookers on horseback on the fringe of the gathering.

The yard sloped slightly and as Chance made her way through the throng to the top side of the fire, the cobbles were slippery from the slight drizzle.

Chance moved nearer the fire and saw people braving the heat and shielding their faces as they tried to retrieve jacketed potatoes.

Dr Bradle stepped into the yard, followed by Betsy carrying a large tray. Behind her came Eva with an urn which she deposited just outside the door and immediately went inside again. Chance watched as Dr Bradle paused and looked around. She hoped he would join her.

She saw him look in her direction, and put up her hand a little shyly. With a smile, he began to move towards her.

But then Miss Bostide, her face tense in the light from the leaping flames, stopped him. As she spoke to him, her whole attitude was one of suppressed anger.

Chance wondered what was wrong and observed the placatory touch that Dr Bradle gave to the housekeeper's arm.

At that moment, the wind, veering a little, blew smoke and flames in her direction and she stepped back instinctively. She heard Dr Bradle's shout of alarm, and saw stark fear in his face as he looked past her.

She whirled round and to her horror a rearing horse, its belly length showing in the firelight, towered above her like some monster in a dream. Its hoofs pawed the air for a timeless moment and then down they came to strike Chance on her upper body.

The blow sent her reeling to crash with her head against the ground on the very edge of the fire, her senses bludgeoned from her.

Giving an incoherent cry, Dr Bradle threw himself at Chance and clawed her back to the safety of the cooler cobbles.

He bent over her, wild-eyed, uttering her name over and over. When she did not stir he gathered her into his arms and took her into the sitting-room and laid her on the couch.

When Chance came to it was to find Dr Bradle bending over her and bathing her head, his fingers stained with her blood. Her uncle was also at her side. She heard Betsy's: 'Oh! Mercy me, poor Miss Chance.'

Then, as Chance fully opened her eyes, Betsy cried excitedly: 'She's awake, she's awake! Thank the Lord for that.' Her body, from her plump face downwards, slumped in great relief.

But there was more than relief evident in the pressure on Chance's wrist by Dr Bradle's fingers. They may have been searching for a stronger life beat, but the look in his eyes was unmistakably tender. For seconds it remained, then it was gone as he discussed professionally with her uncle what was to be done next.

Chance cherished that look, the depth of feeling shown penetrating her mind despite the pain and shock of the accident.

Later, her wounds dressed, she lay in bed but unable to sleep. Her head was sore and her body felt painfully bruised. But her mind, dulled until then with shock, was now recovering quickly. She remembered Dr Bradle's use of her first name when he had tried to warn her about the horse, and the look on his face when he was tending her wounds. She dare not admit to the feelings he aroused in her.

Chance sighed sadly, feeling low in spirit. Soon she would have to return to London and her parents. Glad in one respect to see them again, she was sorry in another to leave Edgestones, in spite of some puzzling and disturbing aspects in the attitude of certain members of the household.

CHAPTER TWO

During the next few days, Chance was confined to bed on orders from both physicians. Dr Bradle would call on her in the early morning before going off on his rounds, and again at night, while her uncle kept an eye on her during the day.

By the fourth day, Chance's condition was improving so much that she spent some of the day out of bed, reading or gazing out of the window.

She was still out of bed when Dr Bradle made his evening visit. She saw that he had his top coat on, and that his face was wet from the heavy drizzle that had set in. He came over to where she was sitting by the fire and surveyed her as he warmed his hands.

'I think tomorrow would have been soon

enough for you to be up, Miss Lester,' he said reprovingly.

Chance shrugged. 'I was impatient and I thought that you had enough poorly patients without having to bother about one who is feeling well again.'

His face softened into a smile. 'And for that I am thankful.'

'I am forgiven then?'

His grey eyes gleamed with amusement. 'As your doctor, I cannot allow you to decide whether you are well or not yet.'

He leaned over, his gentle hands cupping her head as he examined it. After a moment, he released her and announced with a flourish: 'Your confinement to your room is over. You are free to join us downstairs tomorrow.'

Chance smiled at his words. 'You make it sound so important, Dr Bradle.'

'It is, Miss Lester. You could have been seriously injured, possibly killed, and yet here you are, only a few days later, almost better.'

'I was fortunate that you were there,' said Chance gratefully. 'I wish to thank you. I did not know that you had saved me until Betsy told me today.'

'It was all I could do.'

'I shall be going home soon,' Chance said, to fill the awkward silence that was developing between them.

Dr Bradle turned away and stood looking into the fire. 'I had forgotten. After a month, you have become one of the household. You are not leaving just yet? In a few days, perhaps?'

'About a week, if my uncle will allow me. This is a busy house, and possibly I get in the way sometimes.'

'This is a sombre house, Miss Lester, and you have brought some sunshine into it. I should be glad if you could stay a while longer.' Then he smiled. 'But no more fires, eh?'

They laughed together and Chance thought how young he became when he relaxed, so different from the serious person he had seemed whenever she had glimpsed him about the house.

A teasing note was in his voice as he said: 'As your doctor, perhaps I should order you to remain inside for another month. I find you still a little pale.'

'Then,' she replied, 'you will stop me from doing something I meant to do before I left.'

'And what would that be?'

'I want to see the Roman Road.' She pointed out into the darkness in the direction of Winter Hill. 'I've heard it's on the edge of the moors.'

'It is at least an hour's ride from here.' He studied Chance for a few moments before asking: 'Do you like history?'

'I like to visit old places, and stand where famous people have stood. Perhaps even see what they saw! There's an atmosphere ... I feel it, or–' Chance gave a little shrug and smiled – 'imagine I do.'

'I know what you mean. I feel the same. But the moors are no place for a person – particularly a woman – to travel alone.

Besides, there are bogs which are dangerous, and when you get on the moors
everything looks the same.'

'In that case,' said Chance with a smile of
resignation, 'I shall just have to content
myself with reading about it.'

'Would you allow me to escort you there,
Miss Lester? I know just where the road is
and I haven't seen it for a while. It still
interests me.'

'I would like that very much, Dr Bradle,'
Chance said tremulously. 'What about your
work? I would not want to take up too much
of your time.'

'Even a junior partner must have a few
hours off occasionally! Shall we say Sunday
morning, and hope the weather is clear?'

'I shall look forward to the day, Dr Bradle.'

'Well, then,' he said, seemingly pleased at
her acceptance of his offer, 'I shall leave you
to rest and gain further strength for our
expedition together.'

Chance stood up.

'And what about you, Doctor?' she asked

in concerned tones. She indicated his top coat. 'You came to see me as soon as you returned. You cannot have eaten or rested. Ought not you be taking care?'

'The doctor is being doctored,' he said in a bantering tone, and for a moment Chance wished she had not spoken.

Dr Bradle must have noticed her discomfiture, for he hastened to add contritely: 'Forgive my rudeness. Your thoughts are kind ones, but I am not used to anyone being interested in my health. I am more used to demands being made upon me.'

'From your patients?'

He hesitated with a fleeting troubled look, then he nodded and looked away.

A knock sounded at the door. Chance, who was nearest, opened it to find Eva standing there.

'Will you want anything else, miss?' she enquired in her shrill expressionless voice. She was looking past Chance into the room beyond.

'No, thank you, Eva.'

The maid's cold eyes switched moment-arily to Chance before she turned away and hurried across the landing to the stairs.

Dr Bradle waited until the sound of Eva's footsteps had died away, then he went towards the door slowly.

'That is settled then. I shall make arrange-ments for Sunday morning, say about eleven o'clock. That will give us plenty of time to get there and back before dark. Of course, I shall see you before then. You will be downstairs tomorrow.'

'Thanks to you, Dr Bradle.'

'If all my patients were as close at hand and as charming, it would make my work a good deal easier, Miss Lester,' he said quietly.

She lowered her head a fraction before his steady gaze, pleased at his compliment but unable to think of anything to say in reply.

Dr Bradle started to go but then turned back. 'I would be pleased if you would call me Edward when we are together.'

She extended her hand gladly, smiling.

'And you will know already that my name is Chance.'

His large hand took hold of hers.

'Until Sunday, Chance.'

'Until Sunday, Edward.'

She watched him go downstairs spring-footed, which was matched by the beating of her heart with its new-found happiness.

For an hour afterwards she sat by her fire thinking. She knew already the depth of her feelings for the man who had just left her, but what were his regarding her? Until the fire incident their relationship had been an easy, friendly one, but since then he had shown a more intense interest in her.

She hoped fervently that his feelings for her would grow and flourish into something much more. She sighed. Was she being naïve and foolish?

A flurry of rain beat against her windows as other thoughts slid into Chance's mind. Why had the maid come to her bedroom again? Since the accident, Eva had only come to tidy Chance's room once in the evening. Had she returned just to see where Dr Bradle was? Had Miss Bostide sent her?

She remembered the troubled look on Edward's face and his remark about demands being made upon him. That was part of his life – an accepted part of his profession. But there had been some other problem, she was sure. What other demands could there be?

Suddenly an image of Miss Bostide appeared in Chance's mind. Full bodied and breasted, dark eyes with a peculiar glitter to them. Chance rose from her chair as if her action would banish her thoughts. She was tired, she must go to bed. After all, she told herself, Edward had been weary at the end of a long day. That was it, nothing more or less…

Sunday came and found Apple, for Blossom was resting, pulling Chance and Edward across the seemingly endless and desolate moors. For about a mile the terrain was level then it began to descend, the hills to the left towering up and away.

Soon they were turning off and making for a hill. Edward pointed and exclaimed cheerfully: 'There you are, Chance! There is your road ready for you to inspect.'

She followed the line of his arm. About a third of the way up the slope a grey patch contrasted with the dark green of the moorland. She was surprised at the steepness of the old road.

Edward jumped down and led the horse and trap with Chance in it to where the ground started to rise. As they climbed higher, the ground became harder and stones showed through the thin grass. Then a few yards farther up the two-thousand-year-old road lay bared.

Edward handed her down and Chance stepped on to the road with a kind of deference for its age and history. They walked up it slowly, thinking of all that had happened since the road was built. The horse kept pace with them, stopping now and again to nibble at the grass bordering the side of it.

The wind began to rise and Chance was

brought out of her musings by the sudden coldness. She wondered if she had been rather foolish to have come in early winter to stand in the middle of an old broken road high on a moor to feel for the ghosts of marching Roman soldiery.

Chance glanced sideways at Edward. He was looking with interest at the worn channels in the stones. Her back was beginning to ache. She touched one of the stones for luck then straightened and looked up the hillside. She went rigid with shock as she saw a man pointing a pistol at her. He was about twenty-five yards away and was wearing a neckerchief over the lower part of his face.

She screamed. The sound was torn away by the wind almost as soon as it was uttered. Sheer fright froze her. Her feet would not move. A violent push flung her sideways over the side of the road. She felt a tug at her coat as she crashed on to her back in the grass. Edward flung himself down on top of her, his body covering hers.

He swore as he raised himself, pulling

something out of his pocket. She was conscious of her companion scrambling to his feet and racing out of her sight. She heard another crack near by. Edward reappeared to sink down on his knees and gather her into his arms.

His eyes searched her face in distraught fashion.

'Chance, Chance,' he cried, 'are you hurt?'

She snuggled against him. 'I think not, Edward.'

His eyes closed momentarily. 'I thought you were hit. He's gone. I winged him. I saw his arm drop. He had a horse up there.' He looked down into her face. 'Oh, why did I bring you here? It's my fault. I am a fool.'

'No, no, Edward! I asked you to bring me.' She sat up, still in his arms.

Edward helped her to her feet, still supporting her.

'I cannot understand it. Why should anyone want to kill me?'

'You?' he said, expressing great surprise. 'I thought it was meant for me.'

'No, he was pointing the gun straight at me, Edward. I saw him.' She shivered and remembered the tug at her clothes as she fell. She looked down at her clothing near her left hip, and felt it with her fingers. The black of her skirt showed through the blue coat. The hole was clear to see.

Horror-struck, Edward regarded the hole in the material, then he cursed and said savagely: 'You might have been killed.'

Chance glanced up the hill. There was nothing under the leaden sky but moor and the occasional outcrops of rock. She touched Edward on the face tenderly, gratefully.

'Because of you, Edward, I am not. You saved my life again.'

'No,' he shook his head slowly, 'you saved mine. I would have no life without you.'

The look which accompanied his words, which were uttered in a heart-felt manner, was the same as she had seen on the night of the fire when he had been bathing her wound. Afterwards she had wondered about that look. Now she knew. It was the look of love, deep and longing.

She gave a moan as his arms and mouth crushed her. When their lips separated, their words of joy at discovering each other's feelings were borne away quickly on the uncaring wind.

Forgetting for the moment the possibility of further danger, Chance closed her eyes. Could this be real, the change from nightmare to heaven so quickly? At last, tingling with his kisses, she drew away reluctantly.

The horse had snorted – the sound serving to break the spell they were under.

'My love,' uttered Chance hazily, 'should we not be going home now?'

'Yes, we should. When I'm with you I lose my reasoning power, and heaven knows I have no wish to endanger your precious life further.'

With that he stooped and lifted her off the ground into his arms. He smiled down at her. 'I am going to take great care of you from now on.' He kissed her quickly. 'How I love you, Chance.'

Holding her close to him, he stepped on to the road and carried her to where the horse waited. After placing her carefully in the trap, Edward swung himself up beside her and they began their return to Edgestones.

For Chance, the remainder of the old road was no longer a stony way of terror. It was a lawn strewn with flowers under a private summer sky. The harsh wind became a caress around the edges of her hood, for close to her was the man she loved. The old road had brought them together. Edward let the reins fall from his hands and, as the horse plodded on at his own pace, he took Chance in his arms.

For a while they were content just to be together, then Chance broke the silence.

'I think, Edward, that I loved you from our first meeting.'

'And I you,' he sighed, 'but I believed you were not for me.'

'I wish I had known.'

'When you told me you were returning home I did not know what to do to keep you here. I was desperate. Once you were gone you would never have known of my feelings for you.'

Chance stroked his face and said gently: 'I shall have to go home soon, Edward. I came only to convalesce.'

'Marry me, then you can convalesce all your life, Chance.'

She smiled at his words, and her eyes filled with love for him.

'Will you?' he demanded with an urgent tenderness, cupping her face in his hands.

'Yes.' She knew she was dampening his fingers with tears, and saw his concern. She shook her head. 'Tears of happiness, Edward,' she murmured softly.

She lowered her head against him, and she felt his fingers stroking her hair.

'If you wish I will look for a practice in London, Chance,' he said after a few moments.

'No, Edward. I will go home but I shall return. It would be a pity for you to have to move.'

He made to gather her into his arms but something fell to the floor of the trap with a clatter. It was a pistol – the one Edward had used to fire at the would-be assassin.

He stuffed it back into his pocket. 'Thomas would insist on giving it to me when he heard that I was taking you to see the road.' He went on with a note of humour in his voice: 'He frightened me when he showed me how to work it. It seemed more dangerous to the person using it than to anyone else.'

Chance shivered, the sight of the pistol serving to remind her of the escape they had had, and overshadowing for the moment the happiness of their new-found love.

Edward put his arms around her protectively and asked quietly: 'Did you see who the man was that shot at you? Could you recognise him again?'

'No,' she replied. 'It was over so quickly and he was masked. But he had yellow hair, Edward, that I remember.'

'Yes, I noticed that, too.' Edward paused

and looked thoughtful. 'It's something to start with. That and a broken or lacerated arm. I'm sure I hit him in the arm.'

Nearing Winter Hill, but still out of sight of Edgestones, Edward lifted his cheek from where it had been resting against her hair. 'Perhaps, my love, it would be best not to say anything about the incident until we have had time to find out more.'

'I cannot understand, Edward, why someone should want to shoot at me. I am a stranger here. What ill have I caused to anyone?'

'You are the last person to harm anyone. Don't worry, I may find out something on my rounds.'

Chance relaxed against him, feeling comforted and secure with his arms around her. After a few moments he spoke again.

'Do you see that bird up there?'

She glanced upwards and then at him questioningly. 'Yes?'

'I am so happy,' he said lovingly, 'that I could jump up and catch its tail and fly over

Allcaster to tell them all that you're going to marry me.'

Chance kissed him. Edward drew her closer, but released her – they were almost home.

'I suggest,' he added, 'that we do not say anything about our plans for marriage until we have decided where we are going to live.'

Chance was surprised. She was bursting to tell everybody immediately, so overjoyed was she.

Perhaps Edward felt her uncle might object at the thought of losing his partner in the practice, but that need not necessarily happen. Her uncle might allow them to live at Edgestones. Still, she made up her mind to do as Edward suggested. It was enough that he loved her and wished to marry her.

She would write home that very night with the good news. She could not see any trouble ensuing from that. She must tell someone!

They entered the house just as Eva was

coming out of the kitchen. Her usual look of cold indifference vanished when she saw Chance, an incredulous one taking its place. She stopped for an instant, then she turned and went upstairs.

Chance was taken aback, even though she had become used to the odd ways of the maid. She guessed that Edward, following her through the doorway, had not witnessed anything unusual. They made their separate ways to their rooms.

As Chance reached her sitting-room, her uncle came out of the surgery.

'Ah, my dear,' he said, 'and how have you enjoyed your trip into the Yorkshire wilds? Not exactly a pleasant day for a history lesson.'

She controlled an impulse to tell him everything. Instead, she said: 'I enjoyed it, Uncle. It was very interesting.'

Dr Lester placed a hand on her shoulder. 'Come and have tea with me and tell me about it. It's years since I ventured that far.' He ushered her into his room.

As for Chance, the warm cheery fire, the table with its familiar tea-ware upon it, together with her uncle's company, brought a feeling of normality and order again to her.

'Sit down, Chance, and warm yourself,' said her uncle, giving her a quick observant glance. 'Are you feeling well?'

'Why, do I not look as well as you would like?'

'You have recovered remarkably quickly, but you have a paleness about the face today. Perhaps I shouldn't have allowed young Dr Bradle to take you out so soon.'

'Don't blame Dr Bradle, Uncle. It was my idea. I wanted to go today because I had been thinking of returning home next week.'

'I see. You're discharging yourself from our care, are you?'

Chance smiled and gave him an affectionate look. 'Actually, I have now decided to ask you if I could stay here a while longer perhaps a fortnight?'

'You have no need to ask, Chance. I shall be delighted.' Then he smiled. 'I think another two months at least will be necessary for a complete cure. I must admit to being selfish, but it has been comforting to have you around the house.'

Chance looked into the fire and wondered at the fact that her presence should be comforting to her uncle. What a pity he had not married. He needed a wife to look after him.

'So you enjoyed your day with Dr Bradle?' he went on.

'Very much,' replied Chance. 'He was a very interesting companion, and well versed in the history of the old road.'

She felt her cheeks beginning to grow warm. She began to pour him another cup of tea to hide her feelings. As she did so, he said quietly: 'You could do worse, Chance.'

She wrestled with herself about telling him of the joyful things in her heart, for he seemed to have an idea how she felt about Edward.

She replied: 'He is nice but we cannot order these things to happen.'

Dr Lester coughed hard, then put his head

back against the chair and closed his eyes wearily. 'No, indeed, more's the pity.'

Chance regarded her uncle. He did look dreadfully tired. There was a measure of concern in her voice as she asked: 'How are you feeling, Uncle?'

'The fact is, Chance, that I never have time to bother about how I feel, but I must confess to feeling somewhat under the weather. I have a cough – it persists no matter what I do.'

He pushed himself up in his chair and said in a brighter voice: 'The vicar called earlier today, and I told him you had gone to see the road. He asked me to tell you that the Messiah is going to be sung in the church next Friday and he'd be delighted to see you there.'

Chance chuckled. 'He's a very persistent man of God, but it's nice of him to think of inviting me.'

The mentioning of the road reminded Chance of a question she wanted to ask of him, but she must be careful not to say anything about the incident on the moors.

'Has Eva got a brother, Uncle? When I was in the village the other day I saw a young man whose features and colouring were very much like hers.'

'A brother?' Dr Lester pursed his lips. 'Yes, I think she has.'

Chance's spirits lowered. So it was possible that the man had been Eva's brother! She took leave of her uncle, saying quite truthfully that she was tired.

Later that night, as she undressed slowly, she puzzled over how she could have offended anyone sufficiently to cause them to harm her.

She put her clothes away trying not to look at the bullet hole in her coat and then got into bed. But with the darkness returned the earlier terror. She saw the gun barrel come nearer, larger and longer until it was pressing into her forehead. It was a long time before her restless mind calmed and released her from her torment...

The next morning found Chance busy

writing home. Her heart, light with the news about herself and Edward, made her pen drift effortlessly across the paper. She went on to assure her parents that she would return home before making any arrangements for the ceremony. In glowing terms she described Edward to them, but adding that she had not yet told her uncle that she and his young partner wanted to marry.

She let her pen rest, then folded the letter and dreamily reached for an envelope.

Just then a knock sounded at her door, jolting her out of her pleasant thoughts. She called a permission to enter.

Miss Bostide appeared. Chance was surprised, her visits being rare. The housekeeper remained in the doorway a moment regarding her impassively, then eyes slid from Chance to the letter on the table and back again.

'Come in, Miss Bostide,' said Chance, feeling pleasantly disposed to everyone that morning. 'It's a cold day, isn't it?'

Miss Bostide did not offer any reply immediately but went over towards the window, while Chance watched and envied the curves of the older woman's figure. Her visitor was dressed in a black dress with a fringe of white lace at neck and wrists. She moved like a cat, thought Chance, and when she was still it was as if she were waiting to pounce.

'It's likely to get worse rather than better from now on, Miss Lester,' the housekeeper said. 'There'll be snow soon. Did you enjoy your journey yesterday?'

'I did, Miss Bostide. The road was something I've wanted to see for years.'

'The moors can be a lonely place. Robbers have been known to kill for money,' Miss Bostide went on thoughtfully.

'Oh, it was peaceful enough,' lied Chance.

The woman opposite pulled at the edge of the curtains idly, then turned to face Chance.

'Dr Bradle took you, didn't he?'

'Yes, and it was exceedingly kind of him to

give up his free time, I thought.'

'Indeed it was. Dr Bradle is a busy man.' Chance caught the sound of a rebuke in her voice, but the housekeeper went on: 'Now you are feeling better, you'll be glad to get home, no doubt; the weather's warmer where you come from.'

Chance touched the folded letter on the table. 'As a matter of fact, I've just written to my parents to say that I am staying on a while longer.'

The dark figure opposite gave a visible start. The widened eyes became fixed in their stare.

After a few moments, Miss Bostide began to move towards the door. Then she hesitated and looked back at Chance. 'How much longer will you be staying?'

'I haven't made any final arrangements with regard to the date,' Chance replied, 'but somewhere around two or three weeks.'

The housekeeper's eyes went to the folded letter. She nodded to it. 'I'm going to the village later this morning. I'll post it for you.' She held out her hand.

Chance made an involuntary movement towards the letter, her fingers about to pick it up and slot it into the waiting envelope. But she did not, perhaps because of the expectancy of the housekeeper's hand.

'Thank you all the same, Miss Bostide, but I think a walk will do me good.'

She felt rather than saw the annoyance of the housekeeper as she opened the door and was gone…

Later that morning, as Chance walked down to the village to post her letter, she thought again about the conversation she had had with Miss Bostide. It was obvious that the housekeeper was keen on Edward, perhaps had been for a long time. Chance remembered incidents that had occurred since her arrival. The looks Miss Bostide had given to Edward, the things she had said – and the gradual change in the housekeeper's attitude to Chance, deteriorating from formal politeness to barely disguised hostility. She had also, without actually saying so, intimated that Chance must not take up any more of Edward's time.

CHAPTER THREE

Chance's thoughts on Miss Bostide were substantiated a few days later by Thomas when he took her into Allcaster to do some Christmas shopping. It was on the way back when the conversation turned to Eva and Miss Bostide. Thomas was grousing over the fact that Betsy was often left by Eva to do most of the work in the kitchen after seeing to the meals.

'Trouble is, miss, Eva's never far away from Hannah,' he said.

'They appear to get on very well together,' Chance observed.

'They do that, Miss Lester – aye, they do. Eva looks on Hannah like her own mother. Can't abide anybody else even talking to her.'

'I realise that, Thomas,' said Chance. 'She

was not exactly pleased to see me when I arrived and I feel now that I am even less welcome.' She could have added that the same applied to Miss Bostide, but she didn't.

'Ah, well, thee being a stranger, she might think you were coming between them.'

They were approaching the bridge before the ascent of Winter Hill. Thomas, after a short silence, coughed and shifted in his seat and coughed again. He seemed uneasy. He uttered a word of encouragement to Blossom, then shot a quick sideways glance at the young woman by his side.

'How do you get on with Hannah Conford?'

'Hannah Conford?' Chance looked puzzled.

'Aye, Miss Bostide. That's her maiden name. Gone back to it. She's married to Joe Conford up at t'White Eagle. Left him when he objected to her being too friendly wi' customers. Still trails after her, though. Rough customer. Visits her sometimes. Big black-bearded chap he is. But I don't blame him any more than her. Half a dozen on one side, six on t'other.'

'Well,' said Chance with a rueful smile, 'as regards Miss Bostide, she gave the firm impression that she couldn't wait until I was on the train back to London.'

Thomas nodded in the manner of a man who has just heard the expected reply to his question.

'She's one fault, has Hannah, and it's a big 'un.' He paused and pulled his lips inwards, then pushed his hat back and rubbed the top of his forehead.

'Oh, and what's that?' asked Chance with great interest.

'Nay, Miss Lester, I don't want t'get sacked.'

Chance smiled at the old man but her curiosity was aroused and she said in serious tones: 'Anything you tell me, Thomas, will stay just between ourselves.'

'Betsy would have me out of t'ouse if she knew I were telling you, Miss Lester.'

He leaned a little to her and went on: 'I mean no disrespect to thee, Miss Lester, but be careful o'yon. She's a jealous creature – got her claws in young Dr Bradle.'

Thomas's face grew red in the cold air as he hesitated, then plunged on in a confidential whisper, even though they were in the middle of a deserted lane: 'She's allus in season, being of that nature, you might say.'

His brown eyes were earnest in their sideways look at her, and then he pulled hard at his hat, to which one more curve was added to its switchback brim. For the next few minutes he sat stiffly, staring straight ahead and serious faced, as if a dire calamity was to befall him for saying what he had.

Chance hastened to put him at his ease. 'It is kind of you to warn me, Thomas, and I thank you. Don't worry, I shall not divulge a word to anyone of what you have told me.'

Her companion coughed and muttered an obviously relieved: 'Thank you, Miss Lester.'

Chance gazed at the bare branches and

wondered how much Thomas knew about the way Edward and she felt about each other. He must have guessed.

She was not surprised at what he had just told her. His quaint expression about Miss Bostide being attracted to men rang true, and Chance could well imagine men being drawn to her.

In spite of herself, she envied the bold sexuality in the housekeeper's eyes when she looked at Edward.

Had Miss Bostide really got her claws into Edward? Doubts crowded into her mind about the reality of his love for her. She felt inadequate and helpless…

Later that day she went along to the hall to Edward's room but she heard his voice coming from the housekeeper's room opposite. The words were coming and going, as if he were pacing up and down as he spoke. He seemed to be pleading angrily.

She had no wish to be caught listening and returned to her own room. There she sat and brooded, yet could come to no firm conclusion about the relationship which existed between Edward and the house-keeper.

But the next day her spirits were lifted when she saw Edward briefly. The grasp of his hands over hers, his slow widening smile and the longing in his grey eyes were enough to reassure her of his love for her. They arranged to go into Allcaster the following afternoon.

That evening Chance looked over her Christmas presents. For Betsy she had bought a many-coloured silk apron. For Thomas she had a new hat, tall and flat topped.

A frown creased her brow when she looked at her next present, which was for Eva. She had been tempted to leave her out of her list, but what she did for one of the household she must do for all, so she had decided on a box of sweetmeats of various kinds.

For the housekeeper she had bought a box of jellied fruits, and a new pipe and tobacco pouch for her uncle had given her real pleasure to buy.

The last and most important gift of all she brought out of its small box and studied carefully. For Edward. It was a solid gold tiepin with a large opal in the centre.

The mingling colours gleamed in the gaslight and made it seem a living thing, as was her love for Edward.

Thursday dawned and she was awakened by the sound of voices outside her window and she heard the snorting of a horse. Was Edward or her uncle setting out on an early call?

For a moment she lay studying the whiteness showing between the edges of the curtains. She got out of bed slowly, the air feeling chilly, and opened the curtains.

The first snow of winter had come, blown up the valley by an easterly wind, the driven flakes making a patchwork of white on the sides of the black walls dividing the fields. In the half-light she saw the horse and trap standing in the drive.

Thomas appeared, with Edward. Somebody, then, on this wintry morning, had urgent need of a doctor. The man she was going to marry had chosen a demanding, and often harsh, life for himself.

How soon, she wondered, could she became a part of that life?

As it was, she did not see Edward again until they went out together that afternoon.

Somehow, away from the house, everything became wonderful between them. They could speak freely, allow their expressions to tell of their love for each other, and laugh easily together.

They passed through the village, which had lights already shining from its few shops in the early dusk of that winter's afternoon.

Beyond the village, Edward's arm brought her close to him and they fell to discussing arrangements for Christmas. He told Chance that he had been invited to a ball at Fletchmire Hall on Christmas Eve. It was the home of Mr and Mrs Stanton and their son, Rupert, owners of a mill. He asked her to go with him.

Chance was delighted and excited, thinking what a perfect ending to her stay at Edgestones it would be before she returned, temporarily to London.

Once in Allcaster, with its many chimneys like headless stalks in a dark garden, they dined in a small restaurant, with their backs to other customers. And they spoke, without touching, of their love for each other. All too soon they had to return, Edward not wishing to presume too much on Dr Lester's generosity in allowing him the afternoon off.

A bright moon made the road easy to see. As they climbed the hill, Chance could hear the water tumbling and splashing down the ravine, a sound to which she had become accustomed.

When they were half-way up, Edward, to Chance's surprise, halted the horse under some trees. She watched as he brought out a small box from his pocket. Opening it, he slowly lifted out a brooch, with a dull silvery sheen.

Edward held the object between them in the palm of his hand, his fingers half curled around it. When he spoke, it was with a sadness she had never heard in his voice before.

'When I was very young, maybe five or so, my mother became ill and took to her bed. I didn't know it then, but she was dying. She gave this brooch to my father for me. He kept it until I was older. I was to remember her by it, and then give it to the woman I loved enough to marry.'

Just for a moment, as his fingers placed it in her hand, the brooch formed a union between them.

'I love you, Chance. It will mean more to me than I can ever say if you will take this brooch and wear it. I will give you a ring later, but it is more important now that you accept this. Keep it and, no matter what happens, you will know that I love you.'

Chance was too happy to think about his last words, or she would have thought them strange.

'Oh, Edward, even if it had been a rough

stone you had given me, I would have worn it.'

She pinned the brooch to her coat, silver upon blue, above her heart. Then she looked at him. 'Dearest Edward,' she said simply, 'I shall treasure and wear it always.'

'Chance,' he whispered.

Her soul was in her kiss as they clung together. Then they left the shelter of the trees and Blossom pulled them up the remainder of the hill.

Alone in her sitting-room later, Chance examined the brooch closely. She let it lie in the palm of her hand. It was roughly two inches in diameter, made of silver and exquisitely fashioned in the shape of a flower. So fine were some of the loops and curls of the design that it was as if a spider had spun them from a silver thread.

She was delighted with Edward's gift, and joyful at the way he had reaffirmed his love for her. As she turned the brooch over in her hands, she knew that it was no mean present to be enjoyed for a day and then forgotten.

It was a real expression of his love for her.

Not long afterwards, still holding the brooch, she left her sitting-room to go to bed. She heard angry voices coming from Edward's room. With some surprise she recognised that of Miss Bostide, raised and harsh and demanding in tone. Then Edward's, lower, halting. It was impossible to understand what was being said, but it was enough that the housekeeper was in Edward's room.

Doubt greyed Chance's erstwhile happy mood. Perhaps, she told herself, it was an argument over a household affair. Late at night? Her hand tightened over the brooch, making it a circle of pain in her palm. Thomas's words about the housekeeper came to her again.

She went upstairs and closed the door of her bedroom, overcome with the tired ache of uncertainty in her heart.

But the next day brought nothing to add to any of the doubts she had had from the night before. On the few occasions during the day when she and Edward met briefly, his eyes spoke of his love for her.

When Edward and Thomas arrived back from the morning round, Chance saw that they had a Christmas tree with them.

After Thomas had fetched a barrel, she occupied herself with decorating the tree. Before long the characteristic scent of its leaves filled the hall, and Chance felt that Christmas was indeed not far away.

The following morning came grey and icy, and while Chance was dressing she heard Thomas opening the doors of the coach house. She remembered that her uncle was also going to the ball and that he had expressed the wish that they should go in the coach and not in the open trap. He thought that after getting hot at the dance, it would be foolish for them to risk getting a chill on the return journey.

It had been found, however, that repairs would be needed to one of the wheels, the broad hoop of iron surrounding it having loosened. Thomas was going to take it to the blacksmith in the village that morning.

But he was going to have a passenger – Chance. The dress she was to wear for the ball needed some attention and she required some thread to match it.

Some minutes later, Chance stood by her sitting-room window sipping a cup of tea and watching Thomas bring Blossom out of the barn, man and beast leaving their breath in the cold air. She wondered if Thomas had had his breakfast yet.

She hurried to the back door and called out to him, bringing him inside for a cup of tea which he accepted eagerly and wrapped his hands around. She observed the bluish tinge to his skin under his leathery brownness.

After thanking her, he said with a shake of his head and a mischievous glint in his eyes: 'Don't know what your uncle would say if he were aware that I were in here. I'd get sacked.'

'Oh, nonsense, Thomas!' exclaimed Chance, smiling fondly at her guest. 'He knows very well that he could not get anybody as good to replace as you. You're a valuable asset to him.'

Thomas nodded in agreement. 'Aye, reckon you're right, miss. I've growed up with t'place.'

She made him warm himself by the fire, and they chatted about the weather and its vagaries, he saying that it was a bit early yet for a change, and that lads in the village would be disappointed if they didn't get more snow so that they could sledge down the long hills again.

Chance had seen them going at breakneck speed down the hill, like black ants on a white sheet, bouncing and bumping over hillocks and anything in their way, to finish in a flurry of snow either still on their sledges or sliding alongside them.

Then hot, bright-eyed and with raucous cries, they hauled their silent steeds up again.

Thomas stretched and left after telling Chance that he would be ready as soon as he had harnessed Blossom to the coach, and would then take her as arranged into the village.

Some fifteen minutes later the coach, with Chance inside, was rolling down Winter Hill. Through the window in front of her she could see Thomas hauling back on the reins, his lips moving as he talked to the horse.

Soon the lane levelled off somewhat and Blossom lengthened her stride, and they approached the last part of the hill before they came to the bridge. The way became steeper again.

Chance could see between the trees into the ravine which had only half the usual amount of water running through it, the rest being frozen.

She became aware that there seemed to be a distinct slant to the carriage, pushing her into the opposite corner.

She glanced at Thomas. He was leaning far back, pulling hard on the reins. He looked over his shoulder, alarm on his face. The compartment was swaying.

In sudden fear she pulled at the window, and heard Thomas shout: 'Get out, get out, Miss Chance.'

Suddenly, from behind her, she heard something snap. The carriage lurched to one side, its weight slewing the horse sideways and causing it to slip and stumble. Chance was pinned in her corner, unable to do anything to help herself. She heard Thomas yell again for her to jump. It was impossible, the compartment being now at a terrifying angle.

The horse, unable to halt, veered this way and that, with Thomas grimly trying to help her recover her balance. Desperately, Blossom strove to dig her hoofs in to slow down the weight behind her, but to no avail.

And for Chance, the former steady and leisurely progress became a nightmare as the carriage tilted completely over.

She was trapped and helpless inside the coach and her screams mingled with the roaring and scraping of its side on the rough surface of the lane. Seconds later the whole coach swung towards the low banking, forcing the horse with it, and flinging Thomas off before plunging down the embankment into the stream below.

After the violence and the noise, everything was quiet except for the murmuring of the stream as it flowed round the broken coach.

Thomas, Chance and the horse lay where they were. The old man had his legs partly in the water. Chance was still in the broken compartment, and Blossom motionless between the shafts.

One of the wheels was spinning slowly. A stone dislodged earlier rolled down the bank and fell with a plop into the water, the sound giving an air of finality to the accident.

The crash had been seen and heard by people in the village and, within minutes, an unconscious Chance had been extricated from the carriage and put alongside Thomas until medical help could be obtained. A young boy was sent up to Edgestones to fetch one of the doctors, and another messenger went to the vicarage, which was the nearest house to the scene of the accident.

Dr Bradle arrived in a miraculously short time, leaping down the embankment with no regard for any injury he may suffer himself. He knelt at Chance's side until her eyes fluttered as she began to regain her senses.

Thomas, conscious but with a broken arm, was carried by some of the villagers to the vicarage, followed by Edward bearing Chance tenderly in his arms.

There, the Reverend Percy Trupple and Mrs Trupple welcomed them, and the Church's doctrine of tolerance and help for the sick and needy was upheld by them that morning. They fetched and carried and provided everything that Edward needed for his patients, the vicar bouncing here, there and everywhere.

Chance, warmer and more comfortable after the intensive administrations of those around her, relaxed upon a couch by a large fire in the dining-room. Apart from bruising, mostly down one side of her body where she had been bounced about in the carriage, she was unharmed after her ordeal.

'I thank God you're alive,' said Edward, leaning over her for the umpteenth time and eyeing her in great anxiety. 'What on earth possessed Thomas to take you? He'd no right!'

Chance shook her head wearily and grasped his hand. 'I asked him to take me, Edward. I wanted to get something from the village.'

Edward shrugged angrily. 'Anyway, he must have driven like a madman to go over the edge like that.'

'Don't blame Thomas, please, Edward,' she pleaded, 'it was nothing he could help.'

'Oh?' He looked down on her, his face still set in anger.

'No, something happened on the way down. The carriage started to lean, then something gave way. I felt it. Thomas did all he could. He was very brave, Edward. He stayed on and told me to jump out, but I couldn't. Be nice to him, Edward. He's an old man and he'll be feeling terrible about it. Promise me, please.'

Edward nodded and his expression softened. 'All right, Chance, I'll say nothing until I've examined the coach. I'd better go and splint his arm now.'

He bent and kissed her and hurried out of the room, a puzzled frown on his face.

Chance sighed and closed her eyes, thinking that the number of mishaps she had had since her stay began at Edgestones was alarming.

When Edward had finished binding the splint in place, Thomas plucked at his sleeve with his good hand, his eyes fixed earnestly on the younger man. Edward bent nearer to catch his words, Thomas's normally strong voice having deserted him for the time being.

'Summat snapped, Doctor, summat snapped on the way down.'

Edward remembered his promise and

smiled reassuringly. 'Don't worry, Thomas. Miss Lester is going to be fine, and we can get another coach any time.'

Thomas looked relieved and sank back on his cushion. Edward left him, thinking that the coachman's words had borne out what Chance had said about something giving way on the descent of Winter Hill.

It was almost noon when Chance, Edward and Thomas – after many grateful thanks – left for Edgestones in the vicar's carriage.

On the way back, Thomas apologised to his companions.

'I've made a right mess of your day, Miss Lester, and yorum, too, Doctor, on top of it.'

Chance flashed an appealing glance at Edward. To her relief his tone was kindly.

'Nothing of the sort, Thomas. An accident can happen to anybody. I don't want you to worry over it. I want you to get that arm better quickly.'

'Aye, mebbe,' answered Thomas dolefully, 'but how are you going t'manage?'

'I shall,' said Edward, speaking as cheerfully as the circumstances permitted, 'ride Apple on fine days and use the trap when it's wet.'

'Apple? What about Blossom?' asked Chance.

Two pairs of eyes questioned Edward.

'I'm sorry, but she broke her neck,' he stated sadly.

Chance sighed and leaned her head back against the seat cushion, her spirits flagging at this latest news. She was very sorry about the horse. She'd become used to it – a friendly, working horse.

'Aye, I reckoned summat of t'sort had happened. She couldn't have lived, going down t'bank like that.'

Edward asked Thomas if he could describe what happened.

This the old man did, and was adamant in his belief that something had given way on the carriage. It was his opinion that it had something to do with the hanging straps, which were used to suspend the passenger

compartment of the coach on the framework of the carriage itself.

Soon they were abreast of the Flaggs' cottage, with Betsy waiting to put her husband
to bed so that he could rest and recover.
Edward had ordered it so.

The same order was given to Chance a few
minutes later, but in much more tender
tones, as Edward helped her into the house.

When she saw Edward again it was that
evening after he returned from his rounds.
She was shocked at his appearance. He was
haggard and deep lines of worry had been
chiselled into his brow and cheeks.

He sank on to the bed, shoulders
hunched. His eyes held the look of a man
under immense strain.

'What is the matter, Edward?' she asked,
deeply concerned. She grasped at his
nearest hand and held it to her. He sighed,
shaking his head and a look of disbelief
appeared on his face, but he did not answer.

'Edward, please tell me. Perhaps I can
help. What has happened?' Rising anxiety

sounded in her voice.

He patted her hand with his free one and a small weary smile touched his lips.

'Dear Chance, you have endured so much. I fear to burden you with my worries. I should have sent you away. I have been selfish, thinking only of myself and putting you in danger.'

Chance sat forward in the bed, her blue eyes urgently seeking his. 'How do you mean, Edward? I am safe. There is no need to worry now. It is over and done with.'

Edward looked away from her. 'No, it is not, dear love.'

Chance bent sideways in an effort to look into his face. 'I don't understand, Edward. Why not? What else is the matter?'

He lifted his head and turned slowly to regard her. 'This afternoon,' he said, 'I went down to have a look at the coach. You thought something had given way on it, and so did Thomas.'

Chance nodded impatiently, her eyes locked on his.

'Well, I found that the hanging straps had been cut to within half an inch, then the weight of the compartment and its movement severed the remainder.'

Fear stabbed at Chance's brain. She clutched at a comforting alternative. 'But, Edward, could not the leather have just given way?'

'I wish to God it was so, but the straps had definitely been cut.'

Chance felt a chill running through her. If what Edward had told her was correct, someone had tried to kill her again, or at least injure her. She stared wide-eyed at him.

Edward gathered her into his arms and pressed her protectively close to him. 'I'm so sorry, my love, that this has happened and that I've had to tell you. Now you will understand why I said that I should have sent you home before now.'

As for Chance, she was unable to think clearly at that moment. The accident had been bad enough, but to be told that it had been a deliberate attempt to make the coach crash was almost too much to bear after all that had occurred to her those last weeks. Ecstasy and love one day, injury and near death the next.

'Who is it, this person who would have me killed? Who, Edward? Who?' she muttered weakly against him. 'I asked Thomas only yesterday if I could go with him. Nobody else knew, though I suppose he could have mentioned it to Betsy and she may have said something to the others.'

Eva's face came into Chance's memory. She saw again the look on it when she had returned after the shooting incident on the moors. Could Eva have had something to do with this latest attempt? Or Miss Bostide? She raised her face to look at the man she loved.

'Can you think, Edward, of anybody in this house who hates me enough to try to kill me?'

For a fraction of time his eyes wavered, but then they were steady and comforting again.

'No, dearest Chance. It is some madman away from here.'

'What about Eva? She's never liked me, you know that, Edward. I don't know why, but ever since I came she's been hostile.'

'She's a peculiar creature, I grant you, Chance, and she has a strange nature, but I cannot think that she would be capable of that.'

'Maybe not herself, but hasn't she a brother?'

'Yes, but neither Thomas nor myself have heard or seen anything of him these last months.' Edward pulled Chance to him again. 'Don't worry,' he murmured, 'nothing else like that is going to happen to you again.'

Chance was silent for a few moments, but the doubts persisted.

'And Miss Bostide, what about her, Edward? I've seen the way she looks at you, and she's an attractive woman.'

Was it imagination or had Edward grown taut?

He laughed, a short strained sound in the bedroom. 'I have feelings for only one woman and that is you, Chance. Miss Bostide is a good housekeeper. I neither care nor notice how she looks at me. She means nothing to me.'

Chance made a move to look into his face again but he pressed her closer to him.

'I'm going to make sure,' he said determinedly, 'that nothing harms you again. I'm going to see you on the train tomorrow myself. I want you to go home, and stay there until I have made arrangements to join you.' He paused, then continued: 'I shall not be able to bear to see you go, but I shall be happy to know that you are safe. It will not be long before we are together again.'

Chance withdrew from his embrace. 'But, Edward, we wanted to be together at Christmas.'

'I know,' he sighed wearily, 'but this attempt on your life had not occurred then. I think it would be best if you left as soon as possible.'

Chance regarded Edward despondently, then said: 'I did so want to spend Christmas with you, my love, and I was so looking forward to going to the ball. How proud I should have been at your side.'

'And I of you,' said Edward, contemplating her sadly. 'I shall be very miserable without you, Chance.'

'Please let me stay,' she pleaded. 'I will not stray one inch from your side and I promise to go back home immediately after Christmas.' She caressed his cheek.

'After all, it is not long now.' She smiled and went on: 'Then, before another plot is hatched against me, I shall be bound for London.'

Edward grasped her ardently. 'I want you every minute of the day, but you mean more to me than any Christmas. You are the most precious thing in the world to me.'

'I should not rest away from you, Edward, my love. I should worry that you were in danger yourself, and be ashamed that I had left you alone.'

'I am not in any danger, Chance. The attacks have been on you.'

'The one on the moors was, but you could have been in the coach, also.'

'It's possible, but I don't really think it was meant for me.' He stood up and looked down on her. 'And what sort of man would I be to keep a beautiful woman by me when I was in some danger?' he added scornfully. 'I would be a fool.'

Chance shook her head slowly. Then she stretched her arms out to him. 'No, you'd just be the man I love with all my heart. The man I want to be with this Christmas and every Christmas.'

Outside it was dark, and the room was in deep shadow except for the small red patch of fire in the grate. The bed was a square island in the dim light of the gas mantles above it. The eyes of the man poised above her filled the room, blotting out everything, never leaving her face. She was conscious of the bed covers suddenly against her back. Then their lips were one in a haze of passion.

A second, a million years – it could have been either – then their dream was shattered by a knock on the door. Their minds, emptied of everything but the enjoyment of each other's closeness, were slow to react.

The knock came again, harder, impatient. For a moment Chance stared up at Edward, saw his eyes coming awake again as if from a sleep.

'Yes, who's that?' Chance's voice sounded miles away, as if it belonged to someone else.

Edward stood up, silent questioning in his eyes.

The shrill voice of Eva sounded from the other side of the door.

'Do you want anything else? I'm going to my room now.'

Chance saw Edward pointing to himself and shaking his head. She yawned loudly. 'No, nothing thank you, Eva. I must have dropped off to sleep. Good night.'

There was a silence outside the door. Edward moved stealthily towards it and listened intently.

Just as Chance was thinking that the maid had gone, a rustle was heard and then footsteps descended the stairs.

Chance looked at Edward, and wondered if the same thought was in his mind. Eva had gone downstairs again. She had said she was going into her room, which was upstairs.

Chance knew where she had gone. To Miss Bostide's room. Perhaps they had seen Edward come up earlier and had waited to see if he was still in Chance's bedroom. Somehow, she felt that Eva and the housekeeper knew that he was still with her.

If Chance had cared to dwell on the matter further, she would have seen the folly of staying at Edgestones any longer. But she was a woman in love, and love builds what appears to be an impenetrable shield against the outside world, behind which lovers can shelter.

CHAPTER FOUR

The remaining days to Christmas passed quickly and without further incident. Chance, having persuaded Edward to allow her to stay, busied herself in preparing for the ball to be held at Fletchmire Hall on Christmas Eve. This also helped in some measure to keep her thoughts away from what might have happened in the accident on Winter Hill. The bruising received in the accident was receding quickly, and she was looking forward to the start of the festivities.

There was to be a disappointment for her in the afternoon before the ball. Her uncle, whose cough had worsened, decided that he would not accompany Chance and Edward, but would stay indoors and go to bed early.

She was sorry and a little worried. Her uncle had not looked well for some days, and he had been very concerned over the coach incident, although neither Chance nor Edward had mentioned the fact that the straps had been interfered with.

She was aware that if he had been told of the deliberate attempt to harm her, he would have added his objections to Edward's regarding her staying on at Edgestones.

Before she left with Edward for Fletchmire Hall, Chance went to wish her uncle good night. He was sitting by the fire looking older and wearing his tasselled nightcap, but his eyes glinted mischievously from under his straggling eyebrows when she remarked how sorry she was that he could not attend with them.

'Get along, Chance my dear. You'll enjoy it much more without me. Has Edward mentioned anything about marriage yet?'

Chance's eyes widened, looking bluer than ever against the deepening blush on her cheeks.

'It has been written on your face for weeks, my dear Chance,' said Dr Lester, giving her hand a squeeze.

'Dear Uncle Toby!' She bent and kissed him with great affection. 'He has proposed to me and I've accepted.'

'Wonderful news. I'm glad, Chance, and very happy for you.' He got up and brought two glasses from a cupboard. 'Before you go, Chance, we will drink to his proposal, and to your acceptance.'

The wine was deep and red. Like her love, she thought. Their glasses touched.

'You have my blessings,' Dr Lester said.

'I'm glad you approve, Uncle.'

'And I'm sure your parents will.' He motioned to the fireside and then chuckled. 'Stay a moment, Chance. It won't do Edward any harm to be kept waiting a few moments.'

She smiled and sat down, thinking that this was a lovely start to Christmas Eve. Christmas was going to be wonderful.

'I shall miss you when you've gone, Chance. I shall also lose the services of a partner,' Dr Lester said. 'It's a pity I couldn't have arranged it so that, when you were married, you could have lived here at Edgestones.'

Chance was surprised at her uncle's words. It had crossed her mind that he, having approved of a marriage, might have allowed them to live here. But obviously he felt, for some reason, that he could not. However, there was no reason why they could not look for another house in Allcaster. Edward could then continue to work at Edgestones.

Dr Lester spoke again. His face was serious.

'My advice, Chance, now that you intend to marry, is to leave Allcaster altogether and take Edward to London with you. He'll soon find another practice.'

The look on her face must have decided him to enlighten her further, for he went on in gentle fashion: 'You may think it strange that I should tell you that, but it is for good reasons. You know that you are as welcome as the flowers in May, and nothing would have pleased me more than having you and

Edward here permanently, but...'

He hesitated, as if searching for words, then sighed and faced her squarely. 'Perhaps it is very puzzling to you, dear niece, but you will understand if I say to you that jealousy is a fast-flaring thing. It can also be a slow-dying fire. I know.'

Chance nodded, but she was puzzled. She was fairly sure she knew to whom he was referring. Had her uncle been more aware of the attitude towards her of certain members of the household than she had realised? Then why should he, as head of the household, put up with rudeness and hostility to his guests from servants?

'You have a happy time ahead of you tonight. Go and enjoy yourself,' he said, smiling again.

Chance rose to her feet. 'Are you sure you'll be all right until we get back?'

'Perfectly all right,' he said reassuringly. 'I'm not alone. Miss Bostide and Eva will be here.'

But as she closed the door on him a few

minutes later, she could not stifle a shiver of apprehension at the thought of him alone in the house with that incongruous pair of women...

Shortly after nine o'clock Edward, with Chance at his side in the trap, guided the horse down Winter Hill on the way to Fletchmire Hall.

They passed the village inn with the sound of raucous off-key singing coming from it, while, across the street, the church was silent.

Nearing the Hall, they could see lights through the trees and hear the sound of voices carried across the grounds in the still, cold air. The driveway had been cleared of snow, which was piled in banks on either side.

At the stables, Edward left Apple in the care of a young groom, then he and Chance entered the arched porch to join the party inside the great house.

The passage beyond the entrance was adorned with holly and mistletoe, and lamps burned at intervals along its length. From ahead came the smell of warm humanity, of roasted meat, tasty dishes, powder and scent.

Stepping into the great hall, the effect of the colours, brightness and noise was startling to Chance and Edward after the narrowness and relative quiet of the passage. For a moment they remained just inside the doorway, near to the enormous log fire roaring and spluttering up the chimney.

Great candles in spiralling, glittering holders threw down their light from the walls. Smoke from rich tobacco made a haze drifting upwards.

A tray of drinks floated in their direction on the end of a severed arm, or it appeared, the servant bearing it nearly lost to sight in the press of guests.

Chance began to feel pleasantly warm and one of the party. How wonderful it was to be there with the man she loved at her side. How safe, secure and joyous the scene was after the frightening strains she had endured since coming to the district.

She looked at the small orchestra of four players in an alcove beneath the gallery, which ran the width of one end of the room.

The music being played was a tuneful waltz, and Chance heard someone say that dancing would begin after supper.

Supper was magnificent, and Chance was satisfied long before she had sampled half the tempting dishes that were to be had. She noticed how Edward attracted glances from many of the women who were present and, in the talk around the table, how pleasantly entertaining they found his conversation.

Once, for a brief sobering moment in the midst of all the jollity, she wondered if he was the sort of man who would give his love only once and forever.

When the dancing began, Edward turned to her and said, with loving amusement twinkling in his eyes: 'Do you dance, Miss Lester?'

'Very awkwardly when I think about it, Dr Bradle,' she replied in kind, her eyes shining with her feelings for him.

Edward bent nearer to her. 'I'm sure that if I do not ask you now, I should stand no chance during the rest of the evening, due to all your admirers.'

The blue candour of Chance's eyes swept over him. To Edward, they were the frankest he had ever seen.

'You need not worry. I don't think many will be asking me to dance, there are such beautiful girls present.' She patted his hand. 'But it was nice of you to say it.'

Edward looked at her and, although his tone was still bantering, his eyes had become more serious.

'Forgive me if I say you're in no position to judge, my dear. Only an onlooker can do that. I, being in that fortunate position, can tell you that, given the opportunity, there isn't a man in this room who wouldn't be queuing to ask you, were I not here.'

Chance took the compliment quietly but her cheeks glowed with the pleasure of it. After a moment she looked up at him.

'Then why, Edward,' she asked, smiling, 'are they not rushing to claim me?'

'Firstly, I'm monopolising you.' He paused, and it seemed to Chance that all the rest of the gathering had gone and that they were alone.

'And the other?' she said expectantly.

'Well, treasure is hard to find and some men won't look any farther than the first thing that glitters.'

At that precise moment Chance was happy beyond telling. Here she was with Edward, and all else was forgotten in the enjoyment of the evening in his company.

'I do love you, Edward,' she uttered softly.

'And I you, Chance.'

Any doubts she may have had earlier were dispelled by the look on his face. She wanted to catch hold of him, to kiss him, never let him go. To capture that exact moment and preserve it, content to live forever in a fraction of halted time.

She sighed, then said rather unsteadily: 'If, my love, there is to be a queue for my favours, we had better dance now.'

Edward led her on to the floor, the pressure of his hand holding hers fierce with his emotion.

And so for Chance the next hour passed quickly. She danced with Edward and, occasionally, with other men who asked her.

Later she saw that some couples were disappearing into the comparative privacy of the passage opening off the hall, and that the floor was clearing. It was a quarter to twelve – nearly Christmas Day, and she and Edward also left the hall. The cooler air was a welcome relief after the warmth of the room they had just left.

Edward's calling as a man of medicine showed when next he spoke.

'What a fool I am bringing you out here. You run the risk of catching a chill after getting so warm dancing. I will get you something to put round your shoulders.'

'No, don't bother, Edward, thank you. I'll take the risk. After all, I haven't far to go for a doctor if I should need one.' Her expressive eyes sparkled into his, and they laughed together.

They sat down on a seat below the heavy panelling hung with portraits of the Stanton family, and in the subdued light managed some discreet kisses. Then, in the quietness of the passage, they heard the bells pealing from the church in the village. Edward exclaimed: 'The bells! It's Christmas Day, Chance!'

The kiss they enjoyed was long and passionate, and interrupted only by other guests entering the passage.

By about one o'clock, after much chatting and wishing everybody a merry Christmas, Chance and Edward decided to make their way home.

Edward made her wait in the porch until he found a stable-boy to harness the horse to the trap.

'They may be celebrating Christmas themselves by now,' he said, with a roguish look in his eyes. He planted a quick kiss on her nose, and she watched him walk across the courtyard to the stables.

Hardly had he reached it when a woman's cry came from its dim interior. Lovers in the straw? wondered Chance, though it had been more a cry of pain. It came again, and this time fear was present in the sound.

She saw Edward run inside.

'Mercy, sir, mercy – let me go!' a woman cried.

Then came a man's voice and a further scream ending in a whimpering.

Chance called out after Edward in some apprehension. She hurried after him, the cold night air striking her as she crossed the cobbles.

The interior of the building was poorly lit by a few oil lamps, which left all but a few yards on either side of the entrance in shadow. She peered inside and saw Edward to her left. Beyond him, a man was forcing a girl down into the straw.

'Let her go, there's no need for that,' Edward said firmly.

He moved forward and the man glanced round. He released the girl and almost in the same movement swung his fist into Edward's face. He staggered and fell, and the man made to jump on him.

Edward slithered sideways on the straw-flecked floor to miss the full impetus of his attacker's body.

Both men than scrambled to their feet. The man rushed forward again and Edward caught him with a blow on the side of his head. He reeled and fell. When he got up, Edward hit him again. The man staggered against the wall and fell to his knees near some farm implements.

Sick with relief, Chance saw Edward turn towards the girl crouched in a corner, moaning with fright. She glanced at the man again. To her horror, he was on his feet, a fearsome-looking scythe in his hands.

'Edward,' she screamed, 'look out!'

She could see the murderous look on the man's face as he mouthed obscenities, and now she recognised him. He was Rupert

Stanton, son of their host.

Edward backed away desperately, defence-less against the scythe.

Chance shrieked: 'Into the house, Edward! Run, run!'

She watched, as if in a horrible dream, as he made no attempt to run away, and saw the curved blade swing. Edward tried to dodge but the blade sliced through his sleeve. He was up against a wall.

She looked frantically about her. A saddle hanging on the wall caught her eye. If she could only divert the assailant's attention for a second! Her hand flew to her breast in fear of the awful consequences of her own impotence. Her fingers touched metal. The brooch. She tore it from her coat and threw it at the figure wielding the blade.

By a miracle it hit him, and on the chest. He glanced down. For a fraction of time the scythe was idle. Chance grabbed at the saddle. Mercifully, it came away from its hook easily. She flung it to Edward. His fingers clutched and held it.

He now had some protection, but for how long would it last?

The leather came out in chunks from the saddle as Edward parried the renewed cuts and sweeps of the scythe.

Chance watched in terrible helplessness as Edward managed to get a roof pillar, like a huge wooden arm with four supporting fingers to it, between the madman and himself in a bizarre maypole dance.

Soon he was forced backwards until he was in front of one of the wheels of an old carriage. Stanton, beside himself with rage, flung himself forward, lunging at Edward's body.

Edward slipped and he fell full length. The blade of the scythe went over his head and hooked between the spokes of a wheel. Chance, praying aloud, dashed forward, unmindful of any risk in a blind effort to do anything she could to stop the scythe being freed.

But Edward had also acted quickly by flinging himself with both arms around his adversary's legs and pulling with all his strength. Stanton crashed to the floor, his hands letting go of the weapon. Edward hurled himself on top of him in a fury, and rammed Stanton's head against the floor until all resistance had gone.

Chance rushed towards Edward as he, taking in great gulps of air, rose from his senseless opponent. He would have fallen had not she steadied him. She got him to the mounting steps, on to which he sank down heavily, exhausted.

'Your arm, Edward, your arm!' she cried.

He shook his head weakly. 'Nothing, Chance, just a slash. I'm all right.'

She hugged him, almost drained of energy herself. Her overwrought nerves gave her voice a touch of anger in her relief at his escape.

'Oh, Edward, you brave fool, why did you not run when you had a chance?'

'I am a man, Chance, not a sheep.'

Suddenly she was ashamed with herself. 'Forgive me, Edward. It's just that it was so awful. I thought I was going to lose you. I must get you inside. Lean on me, my love.'

As she helped him to regain his feet, she saw the girl come fearfully, with hesitant steps, towards them. The sheer violence of Edward's encounter with the man had, it appeared, shocked her almost as much as the actual assault on herself.

To Chance it seemed ages since she had heard her scream for the first time, and yet it had not been long since Edward had entered the stables. Where had the peaceful bonhomie, the gaiety, the well-wishing, gone?

'Thank you, sir,' the girl said tearfully. 'I couldn't have held out much longer.'

Chance recognised her as one of the maidservants.

'It's over now, you've nothing to fear,' Edward said brusquely. 'Go and tell the stable-boys to harness my horse to the trap, and to be sharp about it. Then ask Mrs Doplin if she would kindly have hot water ready for me.' He added, with a glance at the man on the floor: 'Master Rupert can be left to take care of himself.'

She departed quickly after another look at the still-unconscious form of the would-be rapist, a look which suggested that she thought he might at any moment arise and renew his attack upon her.

Chance helped Edward into the house. His jacket was torn, his trousers dirty, and blood ran down the back of his hand to drip a trail from stables to porch.

The news spread and a shocked household and the remaining guests gathered as Edward had his wound bathed and dressed in the kitchen.

Mr Stanton and his wife were distressed, and abject and profuse in their apologies. They insisted that Chance and Edward should be taken home in their coach, and that Apple and the trap would follow after.

It was just as the carriage was about to move off that Chance remembered her brooch.

'Wait, please, Edward. I shall not be long,'

she said, opening the carriage door and stepping down.

'Where are you going?' he asked.

'My brooch, it's in the stables. I'll explain in a minute.'

She shut the door and made for the coach house. Even though she was in full view of Edward and the coachman, Chance still approached it nervously.

She forced herself to go inside. All was quiet.

The glint of metal caught her eye. The scythe still leaned against the wheel. The saddle, hacked, tufted and bloodstained, lay on the floor where it had fallen.

She began to search the ground near the supporting pillar. The brooch had hit the man, so it could not have gone far.

Her fingers touched metal. It was the brooch! To her dismay, it was broken. The top right-hand corner, part of a finely-created petal, was missing. She renewed her search and she was rewarded by finding the detached part.

On the way to Edgestones, Chance told Edward how the brooch had come to be broken, he not having realised what it was that had made his attacker hesitate.

'I'm sorry it's broken,' she said, 'but I could think of nothing else to do.'

Edward drew her into the crook of his uninjured arm. 'I shall take it to the best jeweller in Allcaster.'

'Rather it be in a thousand pieces than you be killed, my love.' The thought of the terror so recent in her memory made her voice tremble.

'You were very brave, Chance. I owe my life to you. You saved me tonight.'

'Then we are even, but we must not make a habit of getting into situations where we have to save each other,' she said, trying to inject a note of humour into her words.

'I must admit I was surprised when I saw it was Stanton, though I shouldn't have been, really. He has a reputation for that sort of thing. I hear women go in fear of him at the mill.'

'You were very gallant and chivalrous, and I adore you and love you so much.'

Their kiss lasted a long time, but it was not a kiss of passion. Rather a kiss of wearied, thankful relief at each other's survival.

On reaching Edgestones, Chance took on the role of doctor, and re-dressed Edward's wound which was still bleeding.

She made him drink a cup of hot tea, then suggested that he go to bed immediately so that, all being well, he would be able to enjoy the rest of Christmas.

Chance heard her uncle coughing. After seeing Edward to his room, she popped her head into her uncle's bedroom and enquired if there was anything she could get for him.

His light was still burning and he was propped up by pillows.

'No, I want for nothing just now, my dear. I–' He broke off to cough. Afterwards, he motioned her towards the bed, then leaned his head back and went on in weaker voice: 'And how have you enjoyed yourself, Chance?'

She hesitated, thinking it best not to tell him about the fight. Better to wait until morning.

'I had a wonderful time, Uncle.'

'And Edward?'

'Yes, he, too. He's just gone to bed.'

'I used to enjoy those affairs. Good start to Christmas, I always thought.' His eyes slipped away from her face. After a moment they returned. 'You think a great deal of Edward, don't you?'

'Oh, I do, Uncle, I do. We love each other.'

'You must be careful of Hannah – Miss Bostide,' he went on quietly.

Their eyes met in some understanding.

'I will, Uncle.'

He touched her hand. 'Love makes us careless at times, dear Chance.'

'Don't worry, Uncle, and thank you. I shall take care. Now you must try to rest.' She kissed his cheek fondly, and finally went to bed.

Christmas Day was bright with a sharp

coldness, and the rays of the low sun gave the few small clouds an edging of gold.

Chance, having overslept, found when she went downstairs that Edward was already up. She glanced at his arm anxiously, the sleeve of his jacket hiding the bandage.

'Good morning, Chance. Christmas is nearly over,' he said teasingly.

'How is your arm?' she enquired.

'A little sore but, what's more important, how is my heroine this Christmas morn?'

'Somewhat tired, Edward, but very glad to see the light of day.' She gave a shiver. 'I thought last night that neither of us would see it again.'

'You were wonderful.' He lowered his voice. They were standing in the hallway. 'And you're just as beautiful as you were at the ball.'

'Oh, Edward.' She felt the warmth coming to her face.

He smiled. 'You're a strange creature, Chance. You always seem surprised at a compliment. I'm going to make it a rule to tell you how much I love you every day of my life.'

Just at that moment, Betsy came out of the kitchen. She stopped when she saw them.

''Morning, Dr Bradle. 'Morning, Miss Chance. A merry Christmas to the both of you. I was just coming to see if you'd like some more breakfast, Doctor.'

'I wouldn't mind a little more, Betsy,' smiled Edward, adding: 'I'll have it in my room.' He turned to Chance. 'What about you, Miss Lester? Have you eaten yet?'

'No, Ed – Dr Bradle – but I don't really want much this morning.' How strange it seemed to be calling him Dr Bradle!

Then Chance remembered her presents. 'Betsy, will you ask the rest of the staff to come to my sitting-room? I've got some presents for you all.'

'Oh, thank you, Miss Chance. I'll tell them.'

And so, a few minutes later, Chance had gathered about her the Flaggs, Eva and Miss Bostide.

Thomas extended his sincere greetings, as did Betsy again. Eva greeted her in a mechanical manner, simply mouthing her words with nothing in her eyes. As for the housekeeper, she was darkly serious, seemingly withdrawn.

But Chance was determined not to allow those two particular people to upset her that morning. She was just about to pick up a parcel when Thomas coughed. In fact, he coughed several times, and if she had not known of his habit, she would have feared for his health.

He then stepped forward and handed her a package he had been holding, while Betsy looked on with smiling eyes.

'We thought you'd like it, Miss Chance. Might come in useful for thee,' Thomas offered.

Chance unwrapped the present in pleasurable surprise and anticipation. It was a metal inkstand with slots for pens in its base.

She said gratefully: 'Thank you both for this. It will always remind me of Christmas here with you at Edgestones.'

'We wondered a bit as to whether you'd like it or not, Miss Chance,' said Betsy, beaming happily at her.

'It's a very fine present. I shall look after it carefully,' Chance assured her.

She touched her own batch of parcels lying on the table. 'Now it's my turn,' she went on, and proceeded to hand Betsy hers first. She gave Thomas his, then Miss Bostide and finally she turned to Eva and gave her the last parcel.

She was rewarded with the merest lengthening of the mouth, together with a brusque acknowledgement by a quick nod of the head.

Meanwhile, Betsy and Thomas had been taking the wrappings off their parcels. Betsy gave little sounds of delight as she held the apron this way and that, while Thomas stood holding his new hat as if it were about to explode in his hand. Then, with encouragement from his wife, he placed it gingerly on his head and stood there looking somewhat embarrassed.

Chance did well to conceal her amusement, as Thomas reminded her of an old square oven with a new round chimney set upon it.

'You look just like one of the gentry, Thomas,' said Betsy, giggling in spite of herself.

Thomas removed the hat with, Chance thought, a touch of relief and stood looking down at it.

'Thomas,' hissed Betsy.

He looked sideways at her and then regarded Chance. 'It's grand of thee, and I thank thee kindly.'

She saw that he was deeply touched by the gift, so she took the opportunity of opening a bottle of wine she had brought. A toast was drunk to everyone present. Chance thanked them all, and they left.

Miss Bostide had drunk her wine silently and she took her parcel unopened, with her. And Eva's attitude had quite plainly inferred that, for her, Christmas had changed nothing.

Chance went to Edward's room, and she was surprised at the change in his demeanour in so short a while. He studied her for a moment from his position in front of the fireplace. Then he took hold of her hand and led her to a chair. When she was seated, he remained standing.

'I've had another look at your uncle, Chance. His condition is not improving, and I'm afraid his temperature has risen.'

Chance turned suddenly worried eyes up to him. 'Is there anything I can do, Edward?'

'He must be kept warm, Chance, and he must eat.'

She was shocked. Poor Uncle! She had not realised he was so ill.

Edward put his arms round her and gave a quick cheering smile. 'I'll do my best, Chance. A day or two and he should be up and about again.' He sighed. 'I'm dizzy with the swiftness of events, my love. I can hardly keep up with them.'

She stroked his cheek and kissed him

tenderly. 'So many things have happened, Edward.'

Then she remembered her present for him.

He was delighted with it, showing his feelings by crushing her to him and murmuring words of love.

'Soon I shall make you happier than you've ever been in your life. We shall go away together from here. Forget our worries and what has been.'

Chance closed her eyes against him. How lovely that would be.

Before she left Edward's room, they arranged that she should leave for home on the following Tuesday, when Christmas would be over...

A cause of further unease in her over that period was the steady deterioration in her uncle's illness. Despite Edward's careful ministrations, Dr Lester's illness refused to respond, and hourly he was becoming weaker. Chance was greatly upset and sat with him far into each night.

The following day, Edward sought a second opinion from a specialist in chest diseases. Late in the afternoon he arrived, a tall, gangling man. Black-bearded, frock-coated and top-hatted, he came in a maroon-and-cream carriage with two coachmen.

Chance waited at the bottom of the stairs, hearing their professional voices. They seemed to be up there a long time.

The specialist, accompanied by Edward, walked slowly down the stairs, grave-faced in the extreme.

'Your uncle, Miss Lester, is very ill. He seems to have allowed himself to become very weak. He has, I think, neglected himself in helping others.'

'Will he get better?' Chance's eyes clung anxiously to the other's face.

'I have given instructions to Dr Bradle. I can do no more at the present, though I shall look in again in two days' time.'

From which conversation Chance gained no consolation at all, and after he had gone, she sat at her uncle's bedside.

His cough was worse and he looked parchment-grey and frail against the white of his pillow. Like a baby born old, she thought, greatly upset at this sight of him.

He spoke wearily, briefly: 'Edgestones will be yours one day. Do with it what you will.'

'But, Uncle, you're going to get better. Do not say that.'

'I am very tired, Chance. An old man in mid-life.' He lay back and closed his eyes. When he opened them again after a few moments, she saw a sad reflective look in them. He tapped his chest.

'A broken heart did this. Not a new malady.' He went on: 'But I was shy even when I became older, and I thought I'd lost the chance of love. Years went by. I was busy with the practice.'

He began to cough. It was some time before he was able to continue.

'Then I fell in love. It was returned for a little while. That's why I understood how you felt when you came to stay here.'

Saddened at his condition, and not wanting to tax his strength further, Chance said quietly: 'Don't talk any more, Uncle dear.'

'No, I want to tell you, then you will understand, perhaps, why I am not fighting very well.'

'You must, Uncle. You must!'

Dr Lester turned his head away. 'Even now I would humiliate myself for her favours, just as I have done for years. Trapped, unable to break free. She knows it, and scorns me. Edward is a lucky man, Chance. I'm glad you two decided to marry.'

'Only when you are well enough to attend the wedding,' she said.

'No, don't wait for me. Nothing is certain in this world. Grasp your happiness while you may. Take Edward home with you, Chance, away from here. He'll find work.'

'I want to see you better first,' protested Chance, 'and Edward does not wish to leave until he's found someone to take his place here.'

Dr Lester closed his eyes and gave a tired nod of understanding. 'When had you intended to return home?'

'Tuesday, and then I will come back in a week or two.'

The eyes under the bushy brows opened quickly, consternation in them. 'No, Chance, you must stay away. Do not return here. Let Edward make the arrangements and come to you.'

'But why?'

'Have you forgotten the warning I gave you? I could not aid you. I am helpless here.' He went on: 'Jealousy broods and gnaws at the mind until it gives way.'

An overwhelming curiosity was growing in Chance. She leaned over the bed. 'This woman, Uncle, you fell in love with. Was she someone from here?'

'A woman's curiosity,' he murmured gently. His thin hand grasped her hand.

Sudden realisation came to her. The shock made her gasp aloud. 'Miss Bostide?'

'The same.' He sighed and turned his face

away, his hand falling back weakly.

Chance kissed his cheek, and left him, promising to see him in the morning, when he would feel rested and better.

CHAPTER FIVE

But Chance did not see her uncle again. Dr Lester died in the early hours of the following morning. She was deeply shocked. The funeral was arranged for the following Tuesday, the day that she had set for returning home. She decided, however, that she must be present at the funeral, and dispatched a telegram to her parents informing them of Dr Lester's death and the postponement of her return.

She received a very distressed reply from them. They were all the more upset because, both suffering from influenza, they were unable to journey up for the funeral...

Tuesday came, a depressing day with a cold drizzle falling on the last patches of snow.

People had lined the route to the church

to pay their last respects to Dr Lester, and some of his professional colleagues gathered round the grave. Edward had not been able to attend because of an urgent call for his services.

Chance raised her head and looked across the grave into the face of Miss Bostide, who stood opposite. The hatred staring out of her eyes made Chance recoil, as if her mind itself had been struck a blow. She wished that Edward was at her side to calm her terrible unease.

That evening, Chance busied herself packing her belongings. As she did so, she reflected how quiet the house was. Betsy and Thomas had returned to their cottage for the night, and she had seen neither the housekeeper nor Eva since the funeral.

Edward was engaged in writing an advertisement to place in his professional journal to sell his share of the practice. As soon as that matter was finished, he would join her in London.

She uttered a prayer that it would be very

soon. She did not like the thought of him alone here with those strange women.

Chance paused in what she was doing. Had she not thought the very same thing regarding her uncle a little while ago? Now he had gone, but he had been ill. Edward was young and well. Chance bit her lip. She would worry constantly until she saw him again.

She wondered if the maid and Miss Bostide knew she was leaving in the morning. Chance felt that they did not. Well, it would be a pleasant surprise for them.

Before she went to bed, she looked in on Edward, and found him head in hands, the advertisement only half written on the paper before him. His tired face brightened.

'I've come to say good night and perhaps good-bye for a while, dearest Edward,' she uttered softly. 'No doubt you will be out tomorrow when I leave.'

He stood up and clasped her eagerly to him. 'I'm going to be the loneliest man in the world when you've gone, Chance.' He sighed. 'I want you with me always, but so many things have happened to you here that I cannot risk harm befalling you again.'

'Let us both go tomorrow, and leave the practice as it is,' she pleaded earnestly.

'I cannot leave here until I have arranged for someone to take my place. I cannot leave the village and district without a doctor.'

Chance stood up quickly. 'You think more of the practice, it seems, than you do of me,' she flung at him accusingly.

He faced her, an angry light in his eyes. 'I know what I must do. I want to hear no more about it.'

Anger – overwhelming, frustrated, uncaring anger – erupted in Chance. The tension, her fears and the funeral had all played their part. Blue eyes blazing, she shouted: 'Very well, stay here. I know why. You don't want to leave that woman. Like my uncle, you can't leave her. That's the truth, isn't it? Then you must stay here in this miserable house. I shall not. I shall go home and I don't expect to see you again.'

She wrenched the door open and ran up the stairs, leaving him aghast at her outburst.

In bed she cried, unable to stop or to think for several minutes. Then she calmed down, exhausted. Shame began to take the place of anger. How could she have said such things to Edward? He was right, of course, about not being able to leave straight away. He had to do things properly.

She lay limp, too tired to move. She would apologise in the morning. She wished for the blessed release of sleep but it would not come. Incidents of the day drifted into her mind. She saw them again clearly. The coffin. The hate-filled eyes of Miss Bostide across the grave. Her uncle's empty room. Thomas's new hat, worn for the funeral.

She must have fallen asleep, but she awoke suddenly. She could feel cold air on the side of her face. Her bed was to one side of the door. She turned on to her side to face it and guessed, rather than saw, that the bedroom door was open.

Her eyes, becoming accustomed to the

darkness, became aware of a blacker patch in front of her which did not blend with that of the rest of the room.

Hardly breathing, eyes staring and straining, Chance was conscious of danger. There came the faintest of rustling near her, and a pale blur of something above her head. Then all was confusion. She heard a harsh high-pitched cry and something fell on to the bed and thence to the floor, accompanied by the sound of struggling.

Terrified, Chance hurled herself out of bed.

'Chance, the lamp, the lamp!' Edward's frantic voice from the floor. Then his voice again, breathless but triumphant: 'I've got her! I've got her!'

After what seemed an age, the lamp flared. Edward was kneeling on top of Eva, who was face-down on the floor, one arm stretched out to a knife that glittered in the flickering light.

'She tried to kill you, Chance!' cried Edward. His voice held a note of disbelief and shock. He kicked the knife away and rose to his feet, and Chance saw that Eva was fully dressed.

The maid scrambled upright, and if Chance had any thoughts that she was repentant in any way, they were soon dispelled as Eva screamed invective and obscene abuse at her. Then, so taken aback were Chance and Edward, that the maid passed between them before they could stop her. They heard her feet on the stairs, the front door slammed and Eva was gone into the night.

Edward clutched Chance to him as she collapsed into his arms.

'Thank God! Only just in time. Dearest Chance, I was coming to apologise.'

She would have fallen if he had not kept hold of her. He carried her to the bed and placed her gently on it.

Chance reached up, grasped his hand, and stared up into his face. 'Why, Edward, why? Why should she want to harm me?'

His gaze shifted to her pillow and back to

her again. 'I don't know, Chance, but she will answer for this.'

'Don't speak of her, Edward, please. I've had enough. I want to leave this house. If I don't, I shall go mad.'

'We'll decide something in the morning. I'll get something to help you to sleep.'

With that, he left her. Chance heard his startled gasp and then the housekeeper's voice.

'I have come to see what was the matter. The door banged – I heard shouting.'

'That was Eva. She's gone. She tried to murder Miss Lester,' came Edward's angry reply. 'She must be insane.'

His steps faded away down the stairs. There was a silence. She wanted to scream after Edward: 'Don't let her near me. Don't leave me alone for a second.'

Oh, God, she must get up, she told herself. If that woman came in...

She pushed herself upright and looked straight into the face of Miss Bostide, standing just inside the door. She wore a long black gown. A glitter of cruel contempt showed in her eyes and curved the corners of her mouth.

Chance stood up and edged farther into the room, then faced the housekeeper. She was reminded of a snake in human form.

'I'm sorry, Miss Lester, that this has happened,' said the housekeeper, glancing at the knife on the floor.

Chance, overwrought and shaken, could think of only one thing – another attempt on her life. She swooped for the knife. In the midst of her distress, she realised she was behaving hysterically, but she felt safer with the knife in her hand.

'No, you're not!' she cried. 'You've tried to get rid of me ever since I came here. You and that maid. I know you have. Well, I'm going tomorrow – tomorrow, do you hear?'

Triumphant satisfaction appeared on the housekeeper's face and she made no effort to conceal it. But she said nothing and Chance, emptied of all strength, watched her leave as Edward could be heard mounting the stairs.

Chance still had the knife in her hand when he rejoined her. She felt a strange, chilling sensation as she looked at the weapon, a sharpened carving knife with a bone handle. It was from the kitchen, no doubt.

After a pot of strong sweet tea and a large measure of brandy, Chance felt recovered sufficiently to go to bed again. When Edward left, she locked the door and kept the light burning. She was still very shocked.

She thought of Edward. She felt that she had brought him nothing but worry from the day she had arrived. It seemed years, nightmare years, since then, with only the bright glow of their love to illuminate the violent shadows which surrounded them both. Some while later, sleep came to obliterate her distress at last.

However, when she arose in the morning, it was to a brilliant sun under the blue bowl of a bright winter's sky. Edward came to see how she was before he started the surgery.

His visit, combined with the sounds of the house coming to life again on the arrival of Betsy and Thomas, withered to a small extent Chance's intention to return home immediately.

On bringing breakfast to her, Betsy remarked on the absence of Eva, and she could ill conceal her pleasure when she heard that the maid would not be working at Edgestones again. Yet her kindly and sympathetic nature made her remark: 'Eva were a hard girl, but maybe her being crippled had summat t'do with it.'

Later, Chance had another visit from Edward before he set out on his rounds. For a minute they clung together, each finding solace and strength from the other.

'Edward, I don't want to leave you now that the day has come. I cannot bear to think of you alone,' she said miserably.

'I've been thinking, dearest love. I know I'm selfish, but suppose I was to ask the vicar and his wife if you could stay with them?' Edward hesitated, then asked:

'Would you?'

Chance smiled for the first time in many hours. It would be ideal. She would get away from the house and yet be near to Edward. They could still meet, and she would be safe at the vicarage.

'Do you think they would allow me to stay with them?' she asked hopefully.

'I'm sure they would,' said Edward.

'But what will you tell them?'

'I shall say that after your uncle's death, you did not feel like staying any longer at Edgestones.'

Chance nodded in thoughtful agreement. It was partly true.

'It might be better to say nothing to anyone else about it. Let them think you are going to the station.'

'I most certainly will. All I want now is peace and quiet, and to hide away until you come for me.'

Edward's expression became one of extreme tenderness. 'Nothing is going to frighten you again, Chance, I'll see to that.

You've been through hell, but it's all over now.'

He kissed her ardently, then said: 'Now I must hurry to see Mr Trupple.' Then, with a wave, he was gone.

Chance sat staring into the fire, lost in thought. Was she going to be able to live in peace? Was the nightmare sequence of events at an end? She prayed in her heart that it would be so.

But, later, all her depressing thoughts were dispersed on seeing Edward again. Looking happier than he had done for many a day, he announced that the vicar and his wife would be glad for her to stay with them as long as she wished.

And so Chance went to stay with the Reverend and Mrs Trupple, hoping that her sojourn with them would not be for very long. Her wish did not reflect upon their hospitality, for they were kindness itself, but Chance was impatient for the day when Edward, having settled everything, would come for her so that they could leave

Allcaster together.

They saw each other as often as possible, Edward calling on his way to the village or returning to Edgestones. A close observer of these comings and goings at the vicarage would have assumed that it was a house of ill health.

Between these meetings, Chance, being confined to the house except for the occasional walk in the vicarage gardens, found the waiting boring and monotonous. Sometimes at night, she would stand at her bedroom window looking in the direction of Edgestones, and worry whether she had done the right thing in leaving Edward in the house at night with Miss Bostide.

Wild, terrible doubts would beset her mind as she imagined that person corrupting his love for her. But then she would be rescued from these black depressions by the good nature and friendliness of the Trupples.

Betsy and Thomas called to see her sometimes, knowing full well where to find her because it had been Thomas who had brought her here. Chance could see no danger in this pleasant couple knowing her whereabouts. It was Miss Bostide she feared. And Eva, if the maid was still in the neighbourhood...

The New Year opened with rain, sleet and an endless expanse of dark clouds scraping the tops of the hills. Chance's mood mirrored the weather, a dark despondency settling upon her.

She tortured herself with thoughts of Edward being unable to resist the powerful attractions of Miss Bostide. Why did he not get rid of her? Surely he could find some excuse? She determined to tackle him over that question when she saw him again.

But when Edward next visited her, he brought a letter which buoyed up her hopes that they may soon be able to leave the district. The letter was a reply to Edward's advertisement. A doctor in Bradlington was interested, and in a position to be able to buy the practice. He suggested a meeting in a week's time.

'Oh, Edward!' exclaimed Chance in great delight when she had read it. 'We shall not have long to wait, I'm sure.'

They embraced eagerly, her depression lifting as usual when in his company.

He also told her that the maid whom he had saved from Rupert Stanton's attentions on Christmas Eve – a Matilda Bubwith – had now taken the place of Eva at Edgestones. Her father had asked Edward if his daughter could work for him. It appeared that life for her at Fletchmire Hall since that night had been made intolerable by Stanton, he losing no opportunity of venting his vindictiveness upon her.

But later in the evening Edward fell silent, his face not reflecting Chance's own reborn optimism.

'Is there something else troubling you, my love?' she asked anxiously.

'My work,' he said slowly, 'is suffering. I know it is. I'm tired, and I've had all this worry. I cannot concentrate. I've heard people talking.'

'But, Edward, there is some excuse. The practice is too large and you need a rest. You've had a terrible time.'

'You defend me loyally, Chance,' Edward said. 'But when I leave the district, I want to leave knowing that I was respected and my work thought well of.'

Chance thought about what he had just said. Perhaps the villagers were more critical now that he was working among them on his own. Dr Lester had been in the district for years, and had been well known to them. Edward was a comparative newcomer. Another thought, and a figure with it, sprang into her mind. Eva! Had she anything to do with his problems? Where was she? What stories was she putting about?

The time had come for them to part again. They clung to each other for a moment.

'I'll try to call tomorrow, Chance,' he said.

'I shall count the minutes until I see you again, dearest Edward,' she murmured. She reached up and traced the lines of fatigue on his face. 'Go to bed early. It is very difficult for you, I know, but soon all will be well.'

They kissed good night. Just as Edward was going to open the door, Chance said quietly: 'Edward.'

'Yes?'

'Do you lock your bedroom door at night?'

Edward gave a short laugh, a strained sound. 'Why? No one wants to harm me.'

'Perhaps not. I pray every night for your safe keeping.' She paused, then said softly: 'I was thinking of that woman, Miss Bostide.'

He understood. 'She means nothing to me,' he said shortly, waving his hands in a dismissive gesture.

Chance stepped forward, her face upturned in an open declaration of love.

'Please don't betray me, Edward,' she whispered. 'I could not live if you did.'

The eyes which looked into hers revealed a man in a torment within himself. For a few seconds, expressions came and went with bewildering rapidity, like the fluttering of a book's pages in a wind.

'No – never,' he said finally with a quick and violent shake of the head. He turned to go, his upturned coat collar hiding most of his face, and she was left listening to his footsteps receding, and the slamming of the front door.

She slumped, her head on her hands against the arm of the sofa, floundering in the midst of her own emotions after her glimpse into the restless soul of a man unable to find peace with himself.

One evening later that week, Chance waiting impatiently as darkness came. She had not seen Edward for two days and she had resolved that if he did not arrive that night, she would go to see him, whatever happened as a result. She was alone. The vicar was still out visiting, and his wife had gone into the village to do some late shopping.

Then she heard the front door opening, and Mrs Trupple appeared, hat awry and breathing as if she had been hurrying.

'Oh, Chance,' she gasped, 'I don't know what's wrong, but there's a lot of people gathered in the village square, mostly men. They've got lanterns. I heard them mention Edgestones, and one of them said: "Let's get up there." Somebody said it was on account of the Bolton child and other things.'

'The Bolton child?'

'Yes, Fred and Carrie Bolton's – it died. But don't you worry, Chance. Dr Bradle is a good doctor. It's not his fault. I'm sure it isn't.'

Chance sat white-faced, remembering what Edward had said, and shocked at this news.

Mrs Trupple's finger pulled at her bottom lip. 'What can we do, Chance? Percy's out, or he would have known. If Dr Bradle is up at Edgestones, I could go and tell him what I've heard.'

Suddenly Chance acted. She would warn him herself. She must hurry. Already some of the villagers might be on their way up to the house.

'I can see his room from my bedroom. If

there's a light in it, he's probably there.'

She dashed up the stairs into her room. Dim light showed from Edward's window. She must get up to him quickly, before he set out to the vicarage, otherwise he may meet the villagers on his way down.

'Oh, do be careful, Chance,' Mrs Trupple urged in great concern. 'The lane is dark and it's not a place for a woman alone. Why not wait until Percy arrives? He may not be long.'

'No, I shall be all right, Mrs Trupple,' said Chance determinedly, 'but please ask the vicar to come as soon as possible.' With that, she flung the door open and ran along the path.

The vicarage was situated around the corner to the square, at the top of the main street. She glanced over the gate down towards the village. She could hear voices and occasional shouts.

She gained the bridge and began to run up Winter Hill. Thoughts jostled about in her head. No wonder Edward had been depressed, with the death of a child on his mind. But Mrs Trupple had said on account of the child, and other things. What other things?

She stopped to look back. Had some lights moved farther up the High Street, or was it her imagination? She continued to run, but slower and slower until she was gasping for breath.

Her eyes caught a glimpse of a tree which was still marked from where the coach had plunged down the bank. Somebody had tampered with the coach. Was someone also behind this unrest of the villagers?

She reached the gates of Edgestones and ran along the drive. A room on the left with a light in it. Miss Bostide's. Chance did not care whether the housekeeper saw her or not. She had come to warn Edward, the man she loved. She would stand by him, come what may.

The front door was unlocked. She went in and hurried to Edward's room. She leaned against the door, almost exhausted, and staggered into his room. He was sitting, head in hands, over the fire. His attitude was one of hopeless dejection. At her entrance, he sprang to his feet.

'Chance, what are you doing here? You should not be out.'

'I think a mob is coming up from the village,' she gasped. 'I had to come to warn you. See!'

She pulled him to the window and they looked out. The whole countryside stood clear under a full moon.

'There,' said Chance, her finger pressing against the glass urgently.

Edward craned his head, and they watched in alarm as a twinkling snake of light moved along the road from the village towards the bridge.

He turned away after a few moments and gathered her to him.

She gave a little sob. 'Oh, Edward, what are we going to do? You cannot stay here.'

'Yes I can. I shall not run away,' he said grimly.

'Let me speak to them,' pleaded Chance.

'No! I shall not hide behind a woman. You must not be seen, Chance. The risk is too great.' He was silent for a moment, then he said: 'I have nothing to fear, for I have done nothing wrong.'

'Mrs Trupple heard them saying it was because of a child.'

Edward sighed. 'I did my best, but I cannot cure the incurable. They don't understand. I did all that was possible.'

'I'm frightened, Edward,' said Chance, 'frightened for you. Supposing they become violent? Where can we go?'

Edward did not answer but pulled her close as they gazed out of the window.

Within five minutes came the flickering of light between the gaunt trees opposite the house, and voices could be heard. They saw a crowd of people congregating at the end of the drive.

Then the gates were thrown open and the mob advanced. Some, Chance observed fearfully, were going round to the back of

162

the house. There was now no escape.

'What shall we do?' she asked in a trembling voice.

'I'll go out to speak with them, make them understand.'

He drew away from her arms and moved towards the door. 'Stay there, Chance. On no account come out.'

She grasped his arm. 'Please, Edward, let me talk to them first.'

'No, I won't hide behind you. They've come to see me, and see me they will.'

Then he was gone.

She heard the front door open and the shouts that went up at his appearance.

'There he is, the quack doctor.'

Others shouted taunts, and cries of 'charlatan' rose on the night air.

'There'll be none left in t'village by t'time you've finished with us.'

'Aye,' came another voice. 'Let's have him out afore it's too late and he's done for us as well.'

At these threatening words, Chance

rushed from the room to join Edward. She could not stay away from his side now, no matter what he had said about her keeping out of sight. She collided heavily with someone in the hallway near the door. Miss Bostide. The shock and surprise on the housekeeper's face turned almost instantly to anger.

Chance flung herself beside the beleaguered Edward. She felt no fear for herself, only for him, and an angry bitterness at this latest in a chapter of incidents which had whirled both along without respite.

The scene before her was bludgeoned on to her mind. The mob was pressing forward against the steps on which she and Edward stood, clogs and boots stamping on the cobbles of the drive. The grounds of the house, usually peaceful and quiet, were lit by lanterns and torches.

Her sudden appearance seemed to take everyone aback, including Edward. She seized her opportunity.

'I am Dr Lester's niece,' she cried. 'I have

met many of you. You know me. My uncle would be ashamed of what is happening here tonight. Do you think about the burden that Dr Bradle now carries? Why are you doing this to him? He is a good man, a man dedicated to helping you. But you want to make his life a misery and persecute him. You listen to all the tittle-tattle. There isn't a man here, not one, who could say the doctor had done anything wrong to him in any way – yet you would do this to him. Go back to your homes and leave him in peace.'

'Go back inside, Chance. I beg you get away from here,' Edward urged her fiercely.

'No, Edward. I want to be with you.'

A voice shouted: 'If he's so good, what's a woman doing talking for him? Let him speak for himself.'

A man pushed forward. 'Whatever he says won't bring back my Dolly.'

Edward turned to the speaker and said with great sympathy: 'Her curing was beyond me, Mr Bolton. Beyond any doctor on earth at the present time.'

Chance began to realise that there were two groups present. The villagers, most of them caught up in something that they did not understand, and a smaller gang of ruffians at the front of the crowd.

Their leader was huge and black-bearded. One of them shouted: 'If he stays, a lot of you will be gone afore t'year's out.'

Chance observed the speaker, a little rat of a man running with the pack, and brave while surrounded by comrades.

Edward looked at him, icy contempt on his face and in his voice. 'I've no doubt, my friend, on looking at you that you are near your end. Your face bears witness to that, but I shall not have had a hand in it.'

For a moment fear showed in the vicious face and its owner looked at his companions for support. Their leader glowered at Edward.

Then a spokesman for the villagers addressed him.

'A lot of folk in t'district are worried. They say you've got a bad power in your hand,

and when they take to their bed and you shake them by the hand, they always die after.'

'That vile rumour is being put about by people who want to discredit me.' Then he held up his hands and said: 'The power in my hands is one which heals, but only if I am given the chance. I have no power at all if you refuse to let me help you.'

His gaze ranged over the faces gathered in front of him. For precious moments he had their attention. He continued, his voice ringing out: 'I shall ask you something. If a relative or dear friend was at death's door, wouldn't you take him by the hand to comfort him, to let him go with the touch of a human hand upon his? Those of you who have lost a dear one will know what I mean, and that I speak the truth.'

Chance, anxiously looking on, noted a few heads nod in agreement, and from Edward's manner as he spoke again she knew he was encouraged.

'Well, that is what I do for my patients

when they have no chance of recovery. I comfort them as best I can by taking their hand and trying to pass my strength to them.'

To Chance's astonishment and apprehension, he moved into the crowd, stopping here and there to speak.

'Why are you here, Silas Thatcher? Did I not deliver your wife of a healthy son? And you, Tom Hollins. Your broken leg appears sound enough to bring you here.'

Edward stopped in front of an older, white-haired man. 'Did you come to see me humiliated tonight also, John Strett? Have you forgotten the hours I've spent saving you from the fever?'

Just then, Chance, who had been watching his progress with great anxiety, was startled to find one of the ruffians within arm's reach of her, a lecherous leer on his face. Suddenly he lunged at her. She, in her highly nervous state, uttered a short cry of fear.

Edward dashed back to the steps to defend her. He pushed her behind him.

Hardly had he done so than he was dealt a blow which caught him off-balance, and he slipped and fell on the steps. The black-bearded leader advanced to hit him again, and Chance screamed for him to be stopped.

Some of the villagers pulled him away before he could launch himself on to a shaken Edward struggling to his feet.

A murmur of disapproval ran through the crowd. It was one thing to come and question the doctor's actions, but another when violence was used on him and the niece of the late Dr Lester.

Chance saw Edward take a step towards his attacker, but then she was aware of a familiar figure at her side, who put a restraining hand on Edward's arm. It was Thomas.

'Leave him be, Doctor,' he advised. 'Don't soil your hands on him. I don't think they're all against you.'

Edward's face showed some relief on seeing Thomas, then he turned on the man who had touched Chance.

169

'You'd best not be ill. I'd break my oath with pleasure for you.'

'Miss Chance, go inside, this be no place for a woman,' urged Thomas.

'I would, Thomas, but I cannot leave Edward.'

The old man started to say something else but his voice was drowned by Edward's sudden shouted words at the villagers.

'Look what happens when you blindly follow such as these.' His arms swept the group in front of him. 'They're not men. Men would not do as they have done. They have been paid to cause trouble. You others are not like them. You're not molesters of women, neither are you unfeeling people.'

He swung round and pointed an arm at Chance. 'Is this the way we treat a visitor to the district? The niece of the late Dr Lester – a man who gave a lifetime of work in your service. Do you realise that Miss Lester was nearly murdered in her bed not two weeks ago? My servant, Eva, was responsible. Did you also know,' he cried out, his voice ring-

170

ing out over the mostly hushed gathering, 'that she was shot at on the moors shortly after she had arrived here? A young lady who had come here to Edgestones to recover from illness. And you are led to treat her like this even now.'

He grasped Thomas's arm. 'All of you know Thomas Flagg. An honest and reliable person if ever there was one. He stands by me. A friend. Yet let me tell you that some deranged criminal among you cut the straps on the coach, and you all know what happened. Thomas broke an arm, but he could have been killed. Miss Lester was also in that coach and, God be praised, she escaped. But still you follow such as these–' he indicated the gang – 'who, no doubt, have been paid to spread rumours. It is a conspiracy!'

There were oaths and aggressive stirrings from the troublemakers, but the preponderance of the villagers made them hesitate to move against Edward.

He went on in resigned tones: 'You have

no need to worry over whether or not I am going to stay. I am leaving. I was going to leave in any case, but you have made it plain that I am not wanted here. Very well, you must heal yourselves.'

Chance prayed that they would disperse and leave Edward and herself in peace.

Suddenly she saw his face change, become alert as he looked back into the crowd. Chance glanced in the same direction. Her eyes caught a fleeting glimpse of yellow hair and a certain face in the wayward light of a lantern. Then it was gone, lost in the crowd. The man on the moors? Eva's brother? Was it he?

Edward leapt from the steps into the crowd, pointing to where the yellow-haired man had been.

'Quickly, shine your lamps over there. I've seen the man who tried to murder Miss Lester.'

Nobody moved, so Edward snatched a lantern and held it up.

Chance's eyes flicked from one face to

another as they were revealed. Then she caught a glint of gold, and she was looking into a face that might have been behind the pistol on the moors.

Edward's voice rang out clearly. 'This is the man. He tried to shoot Miss Lester soon after she came, and he is Eva's brother, is he not?'

The man's eyes narrowed to slits as he stood, fists on hips. He spat at Edward's feet. 'You're loose in t'head.'

It was a desperate gamble by Edward. He could be wrong, Chance thought. Yet if he were Eva's brother, perhaps some people might swing in sympathy to his side. But how could he prove that the assailant was the man standing before him?

Edward wasted no time supplying the answer to her thought.

'After this creature shot at Miss Lester, he sought to escape on his horse, but I managed to get a shot at him and hit him in the left arm. There will be a scar.'

He paused and surveyed the faces around

him, then continued: 'If there is no scar I will say no more, and he will have nothing to fear, but if there is…'

Chance knew that even if there was a scar it would not be conclusive proof, but she guessed that he was hoping that Eva's brother would be provoked into giving himself away.

'Take off your jacket,' he ordered fiercely.

The man swore and refused.

'In that case,' said Edward, 'you're hiding something and you must be guilty.'

At this the other replied: 'What's up with thee? I never go on t'moors, so it couldn't have been me.'

'We'll soon see. Off with the jacket,' commanded Edward.

'Aye,' echoed those around, 'let's see. Get it off, lad.'

Slowly he took off his jacket and stood holding it, but making no attempt to bare his arm.

'Undo your sleeve.' Edward's voice was like the crack of a whip, and the look which the man gave him as he began to roll up his sleeve was venomous.

'Bring another lamp nearer,' ordered Edward, and grasped the left arm of the yellow-haired man roughly. There, on the outside of the elbow and running from just above it to a point below, was the dark outline of a scar.

Triumphantly, Edward pushed the arm towards those near by and cried out: 'See! There is the proof. This is the man.'

Those people able to see nodded their heads and shouted in agreement. Then if anybody had doubts as to the man's guilt, it was dispelled as he suddenly hit Edward in the face with his free arm and fled towards the drive gates.

Perhaps it was the shiny cobbles that he slipped on. Down he went, but regained his feet quickly. However, the brief halt in his flight had been sufficient for Edward to catch up with him. He grasped his adversary and swung him round and hammered a blow savagely to his face. Before the yellow-haired man fell, he was caught with a second blow. He slumped to the floor, and Edward stood over him, breathing heavily.

'Now,' he cried, 'tell everybody that it was you who shot at Miss Lester. Go on, tell them.'

All the bluster was gone from the man. 'It was Eva's fault,' he muttered. 'She talked me into doing it. But it were her what cut the coach straps.'

Chance, almost sick with relief at his admission, saw him trussed up and carried to the barn until he could be dealt with later by the authorities. The majority of the villagers were now in sympathy with Edward, and she thought that they would go home. The violence, it seemed, was over.

CHAPTER SIX

Just then, a movement at the end of the drive caught her attention, and she discerned a horseman.

Chance gasped as she saw his face. It was Rupert Stanton, who had attacked Edward in the barn on Christmas Eve. Most of those present were employed by his father at the mill.

He addressed Edward in a sneering drawling tone.

'Resorting to violence again, Bradle, I see. It seems to be a strong point of yours, bullying people. You frightened that poor wretch into admitting something he didn't do.' He stood up in his stirrups so that he overlooked everyone. 'Dear people,' he went on, 'I have your welfare at heart. Don't let him sway you from what you were going to do.

Run him from the village before it is too late.'

Chance flung herself forward and spread her arms wide. 'A lot of you work at the mill owned by this man's father. You dare not say what you think because of your jobs, but I can speak without fear of what I have seen since I came here.'

She pointed an arm like an avenging spear at Stanton.

'He talks so glibly of your welfare, yet he is the very man who keeps you downtrodden and poor. You work long hours for a pittance. Your children suffer – they do not get enough food. Some have died, not because of Mr Bradle's treatment, but because Stanton pays you wages which no man should have to accept.'

She paused to gulp a breath, then carried on with great emotion: 'You came here tonight misguided. Stanton is the man indirectly responsible, sitting there on his horse, cosseted and pampered. And he tried to kill Dr Bradle on Christmas Eve.'

'Do not listen to her or that philandering swine,' Stanton shouted. 'They seem obsessed with the idea that everyone is out to murder them. Get them out, I tell you. Don't listen to their lies.'

'I have said I am going,' Edward told the mob. 'You have all got what you came for, but Miss Lester speaks the truth. That idle spender of money gained from your hard work did try to murder me when I stopped him from raping one of the maids at Fletchmire Hall. He called me a philandering swine – ill-chosen words from such as he!'

'By God, Bradle,' screamed Stanton, 'you've gone too far this time! You'll pay for that in prison. I'll see you do.'

His face was convulsed with rage, and his fingers played with the whip that he held.

Then he laughed, a high, mirthless, cruel sound, and looked down on Chance. 'You'd better say good-bye to your bed-mate. You won't see much more of him.'

She stood aghast and sickened, her hand to her lips, as if by doing that she could retract the words that Stanton had uttered. Inwardly she felt as if her heart had been scored with a hot iron.

Then to Chance's complete surprise, Matilda Bubwith's father, who had got mixed up with the crowd as he came to fetch his daughter home from work, rushed forward. 'Stanton lies,' he shouted. 'He would have had his way with my Matilda if Dr Bradle hadn't rescued her. Aye, and he did his best to kill the good doctor for spoiling his fun. That's why I brought my Matilda here to work. Here, where she is safe.'

Stanton looked around him wildly. Shouts of anger went up. Some of the villagers, their aggression newly directed, began to move towards him.

Matilda's father tore savagely at Stanton in an effort to unseat him from his horse, and cursing him all the while for molesting his daughter.

Stanton, panicked, lost his senses. He rained blows with his whip on the unprotected head and face of Mr Bubwith.

'That'll teach you to lay hands on your betters, you dirty scum,' he snarled, punctuating each word with a savage blow. Blood spurted from Mr Bubwith's head and he crumpled to the ground, while Stanton glared at all about him.

For an instant nobody moved. Then they went for him. He swung his whip furiously at them, but he was pulled from his mount and was lost to sight under a scrum of bodies.

Matilda was kneeling by her father, crying and patting his face. All was confusion as Edward shouted at those on top of Stanton to stop or they would kill him. He tried to heave his way through, but no heed was paid to him and Stanton's cries were becoming feeble.

A voice with the resonance and power of many Sundays in the pulpit cut through the confusion. Through the crowd, Chance caught sight of the Reverend Percy Trupple.

'You know what the Lord sayeth,' he boomed. 'Thou shalt not kill, and yet you are like hounds after an injured fox. Stand back, I say.'

The circle of men widened and opened slowly to reveal the figure of Stanton lying on the ground.

'If he has done evil, he will be punished. There is a far more important court where we shall all stand trial when our time comes,' Mr Trupple assured the mob.

He caught sight of Chance and Edward trying to get Matilda's father inside the house. He joined them, his relief at finding them safe very evident.

'I came as quickly as I could. I had no idea what was happening until I got the message from Mrs Trupple,' he said.

'I'm more than pleased to see you, Vicar,' replied Edward warmly.

'Edward's friends have been in short supply tonight,' added Chance, crying a little.

'There is,' said the vicar very solemnly, and with complete disregard for the disorder around him, 'always one friend we can call on at any time, and He will answer.'

Just then, fighting broke out between some of the villagers and the gang of trouble-makers. Chance was hurried into the house by Edward, leaving the vicar to harangue those taking part.

Matilda bathed her father's wounds, aided by one of his friends. Edward found on examination that Mr Bubwith had a broken nose and a badly bruised face. He consoled the young maid by telling her that her father was in no danger and, in an effort to take her mind off him, she was sent to make a pot of tea.

Then, followed anxiously by Chance, Edward went out again. To her immense relief, things were quietening down. The fighting had finished, the gang having dis-appeared. The vicar was talking to Thomas, and a discussion appeared to be taking place among the villagers.

There was no sign of Stanton, and Chance heard later that some of the rougher element among the villagers had tied him to his horse and sent it and Stanton to find their own way home.

As for Eva's brother, still in the barn, he was to be taken to the cells in Allcaster first thing next morning to face a charge of attempted murder.

Edward brought Thomas and the vicar inside, and tea was served to all, including Miss Bostide. Her brooding gaze never left Chance, and the latter realised with a new shock that though she and Edward had won a victory tonight, her real enemy was still under the roof of Edgestones.

After a few minutes of comparative quiet outside, a new clamouring was heard, and Edward went to the door to find the villagers calling for him. On his appearance, they began to shout: 'Stay with us. Don't go away. Be our doctor again,' and the like.

He, after the fearsome strains of the day and overcome at this turn of events in his favour, could not answer them. But Chance, at his side, spoke for him, and thanked them.

As they turned together to re-enter the

house, she grasped his hands in joyful relief.

'Did you hear that, Edward? They want you to stay,' but he could only nod.

Those remaining began to drift away. Only Thomas's trampled flowerbeds and the stains of blood upon the cobblestones were left to show of the violence and passion that had been at Edgestones that night.

Not long afterwards, Edward took Chance back to the vicarage, followed by the vicar with Matilda and her father.

On the way, she shivered, and Edward pulled her more closely to him. 'Thank God it's all over now,' he said. 'I should never have allowed you to get involved in this matter.'

'I was frightened for you. I wanted to be with you,' Chance murmured against him.

'The way in which you faced those people and defended me – the things you said. I shall never forget, Chance my love.' He paused, overcome by emotion, then went on: 'I am not really worthy of your love.'

'I believe you are, Edward.' She cuddled

closer to him, shivering both at the night's memories and its cold air.

'I should have been lost without you, Chance. You gave me courage.'

He let go of the reins and embraced her and, during their kiss, it seemed to her as if their two souls merged into one...

It was well into the early hours of the morning before Edward left the vicarage. On arriving, they had been given hot drinks by Mrs Trupple while they warmed themselves before a large fire. Then the vicar had rejoined them, after depositing Mr Bubwith and his daughter at their home.

Afterwards when the Reverend and Mrs Trupple had retired to bed, the young couple continued to discuss the prospects for the future.

Chance saw the strain of the past few hours beginning to ease from Edward's face, and she was glad and thankful. It had been a terrible ordeal for him, and one which she herself would not like to have to go through again.

When she saw him off, she continued to wave long after he was lost to sight. Happy as she now was, there remained within her a grave disquiet at the thought of him returning to Edgestones to spend the rest of the night under the same roof as Miss Bostide.

For some time Chance remained by the fire, deep in thought.

She was very tired but reluctant to leave the fireside. She drew the couch nearer. Strangely, she felt hot and yet cold. She shivered, then drew her coat around her. She would go up to bed in a moment. Just a few more minutes in front of the warmth…

In the morning, the vicar and his wife found her on the couch before the last embers of the fire. They persuaded her to go to bed. They then plied her with hot drinks after she had refused anything to eat, and hoped as the day wore on that she would feel better. But by mid-afternoon her condition had worsened, she being feverish and sweating profusely.

It was decided that Edward should be

contacted as quickly as possible, even though they knew he would be coming to see her later. But the matter was urgent, so the vicar set off to find him.

Before going up to Edgestones, he asked in the village shops whether anyone had seen anything of Dr Bradle. The vicar was lucky, for the grocer thought that the doctor was visiting Mrs Turton at the other end of the village. The vicar hurried off.

He found Edward just on the point of leaving Mrs Turton's, and observed how dreadfully tired he looked. Edward, up till then, had had a more encouraging day, patients asking him anxiously whether he was really going to leave, and some extending their apologies and expressing their sympathy for what had happened the night before. To avoid explanations, he had told them that he was still considering the matter of his future.

But on receiving the vicar's urgent message, a fearful anxiety took hold of Edward. He jumped into the trap, hardly giving the vicar time to take his seat, before urging the horse away quickly.

A short time later, Edward was leaning over Chance, cursing himself for being a thoughtless, selfish fool. He remembered how the night before she had stood bareheaded and coatless at his side in the cold. Whatever his own troubles had been, he should have looked after her better than he had.

Chance turned her head to find his haggard and grievously worried face above her.

'I'm so glad you've come, Edward,' she murmured huskily. She reached out her hand to touch him. 'I'm sorry I'm like this. You've enough to do. Silly of me.'

He turned away so that she may not see the fright in his eyes. He said mechanically: 'Don't worry, my love, you'll be fine. A few days and then...'

He tried to give a reassuring smile, but his lips felt stiff and not under control. He knew she must not be left alone for a moment. He took hold of her hands and steeled himself for the struggle ahead.

And so, involved in a desperate fight to halt the illness, he spent that night and several subsequent nights at Chance's bedside, waiting and watching for signs of improvement. He felt he dare not shut his eyes for fear of failing her.

Turns were taken by the vicar and his wife, and also by a nun – Sister Annice from the nearby convent, in whom Edward had a lot of faith. She had aided him on other occasions when patients could not be left by themselves.

But one dawn, when Chance's condition had worsened, Edward, hollow-eyed, swore and railed against God, who was allowing his beloved to be taken from him. He called her name over and over in an effort to stop her soul flying from this earth.

The vicar was appalled and shocked at this savage blasphemy under his roof. But he understood, and was deeply sorry that he was not empowered to work a miracle himself.

Chance was just one of many victims of an influenza epidemic that swept the entire district.

Eva's brother, awaiting trial in gaol, was stricken. His condition, like Chance's, worsened to pneumonia, from which he died.

As for Chance herself, she lived in flashes of light followed by darkness.

Then came the crisis in her illness. The vicar and Sister Annice prayed with an intensity which left them limp and exhausted, while Edward stood by helplessly, knowing that he could do no more.

Betsy and Thomas, needless to say, were constant callers, upset and saddened at her condition, and lamenting that Edgestones seemed so different without her.

But one person remained at Edgestones and was not a caller or anxious enquirer after Chance's health. That person stood for the most part in Edward's room, looking down at the vicarage, and, had he seen it, he would have been very concerned at the expression on Miss Bostide's face.

Early one evening, Edward sat weary by Chance's bedside, her hand clasping his. Across the bed sat Sister Annice, tired and lined of face herself, but looking down at the young woman with eyes that Edward thought were the most compassionate he had ever seen.

Mrs Trupple was in the kitchen filling one of the earthenware bedwarmers, while her husband, unwilling on this occasion, had gone to his church to conduct Evensong.

Chance opened her eyes. They closed again, it seemed of their own accord. A name filtered into her awakening mind. A slight frown appeared. Where was he? She stirred slightly. A whispered call was heard in that quiet room.

'Edward.'

Sister Annice shook Edward's shoulders urgently, excitedly. 'She is calling for you, Dr Bradle!'

Edward's face came into Chance's view. Immeasurable relief and joy came to her. He was there. She smiled her love briefly at him and saw his look, which he was unable to translate into words. She felt her hand held flat against his heart, then his lips touched her fingers. Her eyes closed. All was well. Edward was with her.

For him, the thick cloud of despair was breached by a lance of sunshine. He hugged a surprised Sister Annice in unspoken joy, as hope flooded his being.

After a few hours, Chance awoke again and spoke, and he knew then that his hope was justified.

Then, after the first real rest for days and a meal, Edward felt somewhat refreshed and more able to face the task of maintaining the improvement that had begun in Chance.

And her condition did continue to improve. Within a week, she was sitting up in bed, but was still very weak. She felt as if she were resting on a plateau of calm, the violent storm through which she had come now gone.

One morning, Edward called in, full of excitement. He had a letter from Dr

Rodericks, saying that he would come to Edgestones to look over the practice.

Chance let the letter rest on the bed after reading it, then leaned back on her pillow and reached for Edward's hand in silent joy. She noticed how his clothes hung on him.

He put his arms around her shoulders and sat on the bed. 'When you are fully recovered, I shall take you to the church next door to be married, and away we shall go.'

Chance sighed happily. 'It sounds so wonderful.'

He saw the colour returning to her cheeks. Her love shone bright from eyes beginning to hold a renewed vitality. Gratitude showed in them, also.

She went on: 'Thank you for being so kind and making me better. I shall repay you all my life.'

Edward turned his head away and did not reply at once. After a moment he said simply: 'I thought I was going to lose you, Chance. I think Sister Annice and the vicar are the ones who brought you through your

194

illness, not me. They have a stronger medicine than mine. I've never seen anyone pray so hard before...'

'Sister Annice tells me that she is going back to the convent tomorrow,' said Chance.

'Yes, I'm afraid I cannot keep her longer. Now you're out of danger, I must allow her to return.'

After that, Chance gained strength rapidly, and became more her real self with every day that passed. Soon she was up and about part of the day, though Edward forbade her to go out.

She had said good-bye to Sister Annice, and she and Edward had presented her with a workbasket. She had also been invited to the wedding, at a date yet to be decided.

Some two weeks after this, Chance stood gazing out of her bedroom window at the gable end of Edgestones on the hillside. Bathed in the late morning's wintry sunshine, it did not look as forbidding and dark as her mind would have it. It might even be a pleasant place to live, she thought.

The sunlight seemed to dull the worst of her memories.

She pondered a moment. It was Saturday. Edward had not called in yet. She remembered that sometimes on Saturdays he took a half-day. Why should she not go to visit him this time? Surprise him. The idea took hold of her. Surely there could be no harm on a fine day like this, she thought. Edgestones was not so far away. She could take her time.

As she climbed Winter Hill, Chance felt buoyantly happy and optimistic. How good it was to go out again.

Dr Rodericks had declined to buy the practice, but even this did not dampen her spirits. She and Edward had decided to marry soon, anyway, and sort out where they wanted to live later.

A few birds sang overhead in the trees and her heart sang with them. So joyful was she, that she would have clasped the already faltering sun to her if it had not been out of reach.

There was no one about when she arrived at Edgestones. She stood outside Edward's door excitedly, like a child about to spring a surprise. She gave two light knocks on it, then pushed it partly open and put her flushed and smiling face around its edge.

'Chance.' His voice was a mixture of surprise, happiness and annoyance.

'Edward.' Her eyes shone with her love for him.

'What on earth are you doing out, Chance?' There was a sharp edge to his voice.

'I got tired of being cooped up at the vicarage,' she explained, 'and the sun was shining. I thought I would come to see you, Edward, and show you what a good job you made out of curing me.'

Edward's face was still stern, but there was gladness in his eyes.

'Don't be cross with me, Edward. Are you not glad to see me?'

'Dearest Chance,' he uttered with great feeling, 'you know I am, but a doctor should never fall in love with a beautiful woman.'

197

'Why ever not?' asked Chance, smiling in puzzled fashion.

'Because,' said Edward, drawing her close to him, 'they never take any notice of the advice he gives.'

She rested her head against his chest contentedly. 'I'm so happy.'

Suddenly there was a knock on the door, and before she and Edward could part, Miss Bostide was standing there.

Her eyes were wild as she hissed at Edward: 'What's she doing here? You know I hate her.'

Chance looked on as if in a dream, then Miss Bostide's jealousy of the preceding weeks exploded into violent rage against her.

'D'you know I've been his mistress ever since he came to Edgestones?' she shouted at Chance. 'Go on, ask him to deny it. He can't!'

Chance, white-faced, turned miserable eyes on Edward.

'I swear to you, Chance, that she has not

been my mistress since the day I asked you to marry me. Please believe me. Please!' he pleaded.

'He lies, lies! It's me he wants, not you. You should have died,' Miss Bostide raged at Chance.

Edward advanced on her, hatred on his face.

She turned and stormed out, the door crashing violently behind her.

Chance felt sick and faint and cold. She could not understand. Her brain was weary, numbed. Her whole being felt as if a sword had been twisted in her. She was aware of him taking her hands.

'I didn't want to lose you. If I had told you, you would have left me. I swear that I love you. I did not know you when I lay with her. Forgive me, Chance,' he implored.

But the look she gave him told only of a fallen idol, and of an innocent faith shattered. Then everything faded for her, and she crumpled to the floor at Edward's feet.

When she came to, she was lying on the rug, a cushion under her head. She struggled to her feet. She must get out of this place. Hardly knowing what she was doing, she stumbled out of the house, just seconds before Edward came hurrying from the surgery with a glass in his hand.

The brief sunshine had gone and flakes of snow were falling as, instinctively, Chance took the path which she had trodden so many times towards the moors, away from sight and sound of anybody.

The snow was falling heavily now. Almost exhausted, she slipped, fell, and lay sprawled in her misery. How long she remained thus she did not know.

Then something millions of years older than herself urged her to struggle back to her feet and face the way she had come. The man she loved whether he had wronged her or not, was in that house with another woman. But Edward belonged to her, Chance. She to him.

She started to retrace her steps, slipping

and sliding in her anxiety to return. How far it seemed.

Suddenly a voice sounded ahead. A man's voice calling her name. Edward. She waved frantically.

She stretched her arms wide to embrace him, and cried out with relief. Only a few yards, but then another figure appeared behind Edward. It raised an arm, holding something. Chance screamed in horror.

Edward turned, too late. Chance saw the arm descend and he staggered and fell to the snow. The figure dropped over him to strike again, screaming in frenzy.

Miss Bostide! Her hate-ridden, demented eyes were turned towards Chance. And Edward lay crumpled and still below her. Chance, shrieking hysterically, fell on the housekeeper, sending her sprawling.

But she was no match for Miss Bostide. In seconds, Chance was looking up into the housekeeper's triumphant and maddened face. How long could she hold the knife at arm's bay? Only the thought of Edward kept her struggling.

Stones. Broken from the rocks about. Chance flung her free hand out sideways. Her cold hand tore crazily at a piece of rock. It filled her hand. Edward. She must. Please God. Strength to lift it.

The rock smashed against Miss Bostide's temple. For a dreadful fraction of time the knife hovered, then slowly the housekeeper toppled sideways and lay still.

Dazed and shocked, Chance dragged herself to where Edward now lay, under a coat of white snow stained red at the shoulder.

'Edward, Edward. Please don't die.'

Her head sank on to his chest. She felt a movement under her cheek. She lifted her head and saw a flutter in his eyes. Indescribable relief took hold of her. His eyes widened in recognition.

'You were coming back,' he breathed.

'Yes, oh, yes, my love. I was wrong to leave you. I love you.'

'No, my fault. I was frightened you would have gone away if you had known. Forgive me. Truly, I love you.'

Chance had stopped thinking now. They were together, and that was all that mattered.

It was Thomas who found them, after a terrified Betsy had told him how Miss Bostide had snatched the carving knife and run out like a mad woman.

But that awful day was not yet finished. Miss Bostide recovered consciousness while Edward was being carried to the trap to be taken back to Edgestones. Spurning any assistance, she made her own way back to the house and locked herself in her room.

While Betsy and Thomas were helping Chance to tend to Edward's wounds, the housekeeper went to the surgery and drank from a bottle which was clearly labelled poison. She must have realised she had finally run her length and chosen this way to avoid retribution.

It was Thomas who found her dead. He said, in his down-to-earth way to his wife and Chance, that the world would be a better place without her.

Certainly Edgestones was. The evil influence had finally been removed. It was as if peace and happiness had come at last to the house.

Edward, recovering from his wounds swiftly like the strong young man he was, told Chance the whole story of Miss Bostide.

When he had first come to Edgestones, she had provoked and tantalised him until he had weakened and shared her bed.

He had been aware of the scandal that would have arisen if this illicit relationship had become known but – like Dr Lester before him – he had been unable to withstand the allures of the seductive woman.

Only when Chance had appeared on the scene, and he had fallen truly in love, had he become strong enough to resist her.

The housekeeper, blaming Chance, had tried to get rid of her. First she had bribed Eva's brother to kill her, then Eva.

After Dr Lester had died, and Chance had gone to stay at the vicarage, she had blackmailed Edward into keeping her on at Edgestones by threatening to tell of their liaison.

Almost out of his mind with worry, Edward had offered her his share of the money when the practice was sold. The house had been left to Chance, anyway, so Miss Bostide could not stay there indefinitely.

To his great relief, the housekeeper had agreed. Edward, believing Chance would be safe so long as she was kept away from the house, thought his problems would soon be at an end.

But, when Chance had come to Edgestones, all the housekeeper's simmering jealousy had erupted into the violence they had both been lucky to survive.

'Not a pretty story,' Edward said miserably, 'and not one at all for your ears, but I cannot marry you without telling you the truth. I was going to, anyway, once the practice was sold and we were away from here, so that you could decide whether you still wanted to be my partner for life.'

'I do,' Chance said softly, and soon she was repeating those words when the Reverend Percy Trupple married them in the village church.

They had decided to make their home at Edgestones. There was no reason why they should not, now that the shadow was lifted from the house – and their love.

Eva had completely disappeared and, since neither Edward nor Chance had laid any formal charges against her, there was no warrant out for her arrest.

The lovers knew that if ever she did reappear in the district, she would hold her peace. To tell even some of the events that had happened at Edgestones that winter would only incriminate herself – and she was intelligent enough not to do that.

But, as Edward carried his bride over the threshold of the old house, neither he nor Chance was looking back. The past was done with, paid for.

They were looking forward to their life together – and every corner of Edgestones seemed to glow in the reflected glory of their love.

This Large Print Book, for people
who cannot read normal print,
is published under the auspices of
THE ULVERSCROFT FOUNDATION